Begging for the Boosters . . .

"We need you!" Bruce cried, holding his arms out at his sides. "We need the Boosters. We'll lose if you don't help." He tried hard to keep the sincere look on his face. "I'm asking, no, begging you to come inside and cheer. Help us win the championship for Sweet Valley Middle School. Take pity on us." He tried to look as sad as he could.

The Honeybees just looked bored. Ellen leaned down and retied her sneaker.

"Look, we'll come to every single game you guys play," Bruce said desperately.

"The season's almost over," Lila pointed out.

"We'll cheer loudly," Bruce said, thinking fast. "We'll come early and leave late."

Maria yawned and scratched her leg.

"Come on," Bruce pleaded. "Halftime's almost over. Name your price."

"Hmm." Jessica got an evil glint in her eye. She motioned the Honeybees over, and they huddled together, their backs to him. He felt a pang of fear. He had a bad feeling about this.

Finally they turned back around. The look of triumph on their faces was terrible to see. Bruce swallowed hard.

"OK," Janet said, a frightening sneer on her face. "We'll make you a deal. An offer you can't refuse."

SWEET VALLEY TWINS

The Battle of the Cheerleaders

Written by
Jamie Suzanne

Created by
FRANCINE PASCAL

BANTAM BOOKS
NEW YORK • TORONTO • LONDON • SYDNEY • AUCKLAND

To Ben Markowitz, Johnny's Friend

RL 4, 008-012

THE BATTLE OF THE CHEERLEADERS
A Bantam Book / April 1996

Sweet Valley High® and Sweet Valley Twins® are registered trademarks of Francine Pascal

Conceived by Francine Pascal

Produced by Daniel Weiss Associates, Inc.
33 West 17th Street
New York, NY 10011

Cover art by James Mathewuse

ISBN: 0-553-48199-1

Published simultaneously in the United States and Canada

Bantam Books are published by Bantam Books, a division of Bantam Doubleday Dell Publishing Group, Inc. Its trademark, consisting of the words "Bantam Books" and the portrayal of a rooster, is Registered in the U.S. Patent and Trademark Office and in other countries. Marca Registrada. Bantam Books, 1540 Broadway, New York, New York 10036.

PRINTED IN THE UNITED STATES OF AMERICA

OPM 0 9 8 7 6 5 4 3 2 1

One

"And he makes it! The crowd goes wild!" Steven Wakefield caught the basketball on the rebound and dribbled it down his driveway. The hot Saturday morning sun reflected off the asphalt, and Steven wiped the sweat from his brow. Then he turned and made a high jump shot. The basketball fell neatly through the hoop attached to the front of the garage.

"Two points! Steven Wakefield makes another two points for the Bulls! It's incredible, folks! This sets a new NBA record!" His arms triumphantly in the air, Steven trotted down the driveway and retrieved the ball. He had been practicing all morning, killing time before he could meet his best friend, Joe Howell, at the basketball court in the park.

He dribbled the ball slowly down the driveway, imagining the amazing future in front of him. First he'd make varsity on the team at Sweet Valley High, where he was a freshman. Then he'd get a university basketball scholarship. And after graduation? He'd be recruited by the NBA.

Standing at the foul line his father had painted on the driveway, Steven practiced his foul shots. If he joined the NBA when he was twenty-one, he could probably play a good fifteen years or so. Between his NBA salary and the money he would get from endorsing sneakers and sports drinks and cars and stuff, he would be set for life. He grinned, thinking of the great house he would buy, right on the beach. His twelve-year-old twin sisters, Jessica and Elizabeth, would want to croak when they saw it.

Steven started to practice his three-point line shots. He'd been practicing these all week, and it was paying off—he made eight out of ten. Now he had to try for ten out of ten. *But a guy has to think long-term,* he told himself, setting up a shot. What about when his knees gave out? What about when younger guys started making all the shots? He needed a backup plan. That was why he was trying for the assistant coaching position at the Sweet Valley Middle School basketball camp that Coach Berger was going to run next summer. Then, when he was too old to play, he could retire gracefully from his pro team and start coaching full time.

Steven could imagine one of the television interviews he'd have once he made it big as a coach.

"Coach 'Steamin' Steven' Wakefield, who as a guard rocketed the Bulls toward win after win, has brought his team into the championships once again," the news reporter said enthusiastically. "Yes, his coaching has made a real difference in the Knicks' performance this season. Why, without him they may as well have hung up their shorts."

Boom! The ball banged against the garage wall, then dropped through the net. "Three points!" Steven cheered.

The more he thought about it, the more psyched he was to get that summertime coaching job. Not only would it be extra money and good experience for the future, but it would probably also be sort of fun. He pictured little sixth-graders coming up to him for advice, hanging on his every word, admiring his skill and wishing they could be even one-half as good as he is. In a way, it was kind of his duty to share his expertise and natural talent with those less knowledgeable and gifted.

Dribbling the ball thoughtfully, Steven glanced through the kitchen window. *There they are,* he thought with a sigh. *The Pointless Sisters.* Jessica and Elizabeth were sitting at the kitchen table. *A beautiful Saturday morning in sunny southern California, and they're hanging out in the air-conditioning like two blond couch potatoes.*

Steven tapped on the kitchen window. "Jess! Elizabeth! Come on, get out here!" He held the basketball up so they could see it. "Come on! Let's get your blood pumping!"

The twins turned and looked at him, and he gestured toward the ball, then waved his arm to demonstrate the joy of being outdoors. *What the hey,* he figured, beckoning them with his finger. *If I'm going after the coaching job, I might as well practice on two complete losers. If I can coach* them, *I can coach* anybody.

"What does he want?" Jessica frowned in irritation. "Why is he banging on the window?"

"Umm, he seems to want us to go outside," Elizabeth said, looking disinterested. She took a bite of toast and turned the newspaper page.

"What are you going to do today?" Jessica asked, ignoring Steven, who continued to tap on the window.

Elizabeth shrugged. "No real plans. Amy might come over." Amy Sutton was her best friend.

"I might meet Lila at the mall," Jessica mused. She took a sip of juice and wiped her lips. "Valley Fashions is having a sale. I could use some new sandals. Then we could have lunch at Taco Shack or maybe Spuds 'n' Stuffin'."

"I see you have a real important day mapped out," Elizabeth said with a grin.

"Well, it's better than sitting around *studying* all day, like you and Amy are probably going to do," Jessica defended herself. That was the major difference between her and Elizabeth, Jessica thought. *One* of the major differences. True, they each had long blond hair, blue-green eyes, and dimples in their left cheeks. And they were the same height, the same weight, and in the same sixth-grade class at Sweet Valley Middle School. But on the inside, they were completely different. Jessica was daring, exciting, a risk-taker. *And let's face it,* Jessica thought,

Elizabeth just isn't. Elizabeth was steady, studious, and dependable. Which were perfectly decent qualities, Jessica supposed. But they weren't going to set the world on fire.

"Hey! Didn't you guys hear me calling you?" Steven stomped into the kitchen, his basketball tucked under his arm, his hair damp with sweat.

"Yeah," Jessica replied. "So?"

"So come on outside. Let's shoot some hoops."

Jessica looked at Elizabeth. Elizabeth looked at Jessica.

"Did he say, shoot some hoops?" Jessica asked.

Elizabeth nodded. "I guess he was talking to us," she said. "There's no one else here."

"Very funny," Steven said impatiently. "Come on, guys. It won't kill you to get some physical exercise."

Jessica looked out the window. It was a beautiful day, sunny and bright. She could see a breeze ruffling the tops of the trees. "Well, OK," she said, closing the top of the orange juice carton. "We might as well. But only until I have to go meet Lila."

"Or Amy comes over," Elizabeth said.

"Whatever," Steven said. "Let's go."

"Quick! Pass me the ball, Jess!" Steven yelled.

Jessica dribbled the ball up the driveway, then passed it right over Steven's head to Elizabeth. Elizabeth bounced it once and leaped up to make a great layup shot. The ball went through the hoop.

"Yay! Way to go, Elizabeth!" Jessica ran over to give her sister a high five. *This is actually kind of fun,*

Jessica thought as she and Elizabeth split up to guard Steven. Even though she had never played that much basketball, it seemed to be coming naturally to her. And of course she always enjoyed it when she and Elizabeth ganged up on Steven.

"He makes the shot!" Steven shouted, jumping up and trying to throw the ball past Elizabeth's outstretched hands. Jessica cheered when her sister managed to whack the ball sideways so it sailed way over to one side of the hoop.

"He misses!" Jessica cried, hopping up and down in excitement. "The blond team pulls into the lead!"

"OK, Elizabeth, catch!" Steven had caught the ball on the rebound, and now he passed it to Elizabeth. "Dribble it to the top of the key, then try for an outside shot."

Elizabeth did as he said, and squealed happily when the ball dropped neatly through the mesh of the net.

"Another point for the blond team!" Jessica cried, grabbing the ball and dribbling it down the driveway. She stood at the three-point line and aimed carefully while Elizabeth bounced around, trying to keep Steven out of the way. With a quick lunge, he reached around her, but Elizabeth threw her body sideways and blocked him as Jessica shot the ball. "She makes it! The blond team pulls into the lead!" Jessica crowed.

"I should have known you two would gang up on me," Steven muttered bitterly. "Could one of you be loyal to your older brother? Noooo. That would be asking too much."

Again and again the twins snatched the ball away from Steven, scoring basket after basket. Jessica's outside shots were her best. Elizabeth was great with layups. Steven played his hardest, but he was no match for the twins once they got going. After an hour, all three Wakefields were red-faced, sweating, and exhausted. They flopped down on the lawn next to the swimming pool and fanned their faces.

"I knew it," Steven said weakly. "I can coach anybody."

"You weren't coaching us," Jessica corrected him, flapping her shirt up and down to make a breeze. "You were desperately trying to hold your own."

"Yeah, and you couldn't even do *that*." Elizabeth giggled.

"It was two against one," Steven protested.

"Don't be ashamed, Steven," Elizabeth said airily. "Girls are natural athletes. You never had a chance."

Steven frowned. "It was *my* coaching that helped you two!"

"Yeah, yeah," Jessica said, sounding bored. She pulled herself to her feet and started across the patio to the sliding glass doors. "Face it, Steven. We were naturals. We're probably better at basketball than a lot of your friends."

"What?" Steven cried, outraged. He leaped to his feet and rushed after Jessica. "No way are a couple of skinny sixth-grade girls anywhere *close* to being as good as the guys on junior varsity! Are you out of your tiny mi—*augh!*" Jessica gave him a huge shove, and he toppled backwards. He flailed his arms, trying to catch his balance. But it was no use—he landed in the swimming pool with a splash.

The rest of his words were swallowed as his head disappeared beneath the water. When he bobbed to the surface, he was sputtering with fury. "I'll get you for this, Jessica!" he said darkly, glaring at her.

Elizabeth gave Jessica a high five, and they both started laughing.

"You and what basketball team?" Jessica asked. Then she turned and glided through the glass doors.

Two

"Pass me the coconut oil, Jess." Lila Fowler held out her hand.

"Okeydokey." Jessica dug in her beach bag for the bottle of oil and passed it over to Lila. Then she settled back on her beach towel.

She and Lila had been best friends—and sometimes best enemies—since second grade. Sometimes it was hard having a best friend who had everything. Lila's father owned Fowler Industries, and they lived in one of the biggest and fanciest mansions in Sweet Valley. Her father was known for buying Lila anything she wanted. Today she was wearing a black one-piece bathing suit with gold trim that Jessica knew had cost more than all of her own swimsuits combined.

"This is great, huh?" Janet Howell said lazily, sipping from her bottle of iced tea. "The perfect Sunday afternoon."

"We should have all the Unicorns meetings out here," Ellen Riteman added, adjusting her sunglasses on her nose.

The Unicorns were an exclusive group of the prettiest and most popular girls at Sweet Valley Middle School. Jessica and Lila were members, and so were their closest friends. Girls in the Unicorn Club tried to wear something purple, the color of royalty, every single day. Jessica even had a pair of purple unicorn earrings.

Today the Unicorns had decided to hold their weekly meeting in the park near Jessica's house. They had brought towels, sunscreen, drinks, and a portable CD player. That was one of the best things about being a Unicorn, Jessica mused as she pulled her long blond hair into a ponytail. They hardly ever cluttered up their meetings with boring things like minutes and votes and resolutions.

"Let's hang out here for a while, then continue the meeting over by Jessica's pool," Belinda Layton suggested.

"Good plan," Janet said. Then she pointed to the bicycle path. "Look, Jess. There goes your *un*identical twin sister."

Ellen and Lila snickered, and Jessica knew why. No one could deny that she and Elizabeth looked just alike, but there was no way that Elizabeth would be a Unicorn. Elizabeth thought the Unicorns were silly—she just didn't understand how important it was to belong to the right social circle. Jessica thought Elizabeth's friends were pretty boring.

Now Elizabeth was Rollerblading with Amy, Maria Slater, and Julie Porter.

"I bet they're totally hot and sweaty." Lila wrinkled her nose. "Yuck."

"Sweat is definitely uncool," Tamara Chase said.

"Actually, it says here that sweating is really good for your skin." Mandy Miller pointed to her fashion magazine. "It clears out all your pores."

"Mandy, that is totally disgusting," Janet informed her.

"I don't know if it's healthy or disgusting or what," Jessica said, "but I was sweating like a pig yesterday when Elizabeth and I whipped Steven at basketball."

"Oh, you did not, Jess." Lila rolled her eyes. "Steven's really good at basketball."

"Yeah," Janet sighed. "Not only is he a fabulous player, but he's older and taller and on the junior varsity at Sweet Valley High."

Jessica hid her smile. Everyone knew that Janet had had a crush on Steven forever. Jessica personally thought that Janet's taste was pretty terrible in this department, but she wasn't about to say so. Janet was an eighth-grader and the president of the Unicorns, and criticizing her was never a good move.

Jessica tossed her ponytail over her shoulder. "I swear, you guys, Elizabeth and I tromped all over him."

Ellen raised her eyebrows. "You might be a great Booster, Jessica, but are you really that good at basketball?"

Almost all of the Unicorns were also on the Booster squad, which was Sweet Valley Middle School's cheerleading squad. The Boosters also had some non-Unicorn members, Amy Sutton and Winston Egbert.

"Sure," Jessica insisted, when something caught her eye. "Hey, speaking of basketball, look over there." Nearby, on the public basketball court, several boys from their school were practicing their shots.

"Bruce is being his usual loudmouthed self," Mandy remarked.

Bruce Patman was a seventh-grader and the wealthiest boy in school, not to mention one of the cutest. He was also obnoxious and bossy.

While the Unicorns watched, the guys lined up and took turns taking foul shots, then jump shots. Any time one of them missed, he got another letter of the word "horse."

"Look, Rick has almost the whole word spelled," Lila said, pointing at Rick Hunter.

"He has almost a whole stable spelled." Jessica giggled. "Guess he just hasn't got it."

"So you're saying you do?" Tamara asked skeptically.

"Of course I do." Jessica coolly examined her nails.

"Oh, yeah?" Janet flashed her a challenging glance. "How about putting your money where your mouth is?"

Jessica wasn't about to back down from a challenge—especially one from Janet Howell. Getting up, Jessica pulled on her T-shirt and jammed her feet into her sneakers. "Stand back, ladies," she said, "and prepare to be impressed."

"Hey, guys. Can I play?"

Bruce Patman wheeled around to see Jessica Wakefield, her hands on her hips, at the edge of the court. "What do you want, Wakefield?" he asked curtly, passing the ball to Todd Wilkins for his turn.

"I want to play, too, OK?" She came onto the court and took her place in the lineup.

"Hold it!" Bruce signaled to Todd to stop. Then he strode over to Jessica. "What do you think you're doing?" he demanded.

Jessica's blue-green eyes narrowed in irritation. "I think I'm getting in line to play Horse. What do you think *you're* doing?"

"OK, out." Bruce jerked his thumb over his shoulder toward the edge of the court. "Come on. We're in the middle of a game here."

Jessica crossed her arms over her chest. "You're playing Horse, and there's no player limit. I want to play, too."

"Sorry, Jessica," Rick Hunter said, walking over to them. "This is a guys-only game."

"Why? Afraid I'll show you up?" Jessica challenged him.

Rick and Bruce both guffawed loudly.

"Yeah, right," Rick said.

"Well, I've seen your outside shot, Rick," Jessica said, "and frankly, you stink."

"What?" Rick cried in outrage.

"Hey, what's the big deal?" Aaron Dallas approached them and stood between Jessica and Rick. "We're just playing a friendly game of Horse." He turned to Bruce. "She should be able to play if she wants to."

Jessica gave Aaron a big smile. He was her sort-of boyfriend, and she'd had a feeling he'd come through for her. "Thanks, Aaron."

"No way." Bruce shook his head. "We don't want girls getting in the way. This is a guys' game. I mean, what if she falls and hurts herself? I don't have time to deal with some girl crying."

"Oh, give me a break!" Jessica cried, rolling her eyes.

Bruce was about to threaten her with the fact that she'd probably break a nail when Elizabeth, Amy, Maria, and Julie skated over.

"Jessica should be allowed to play," Elizabeth declared. "Unless, of course, you're afraid."

Bruce glared at her. Why were girls such a big pain in the neck? "Fine," he said shortly. He grabbed the ball from Todd and threw it hard at Jessica. "Play if you want."

Jessica caught the ball expertly and went to the front of the line. "Outside shots, right?" she said. She took aim, bent her knees, then sprang up and released the ball. It flew in a graceful arc toward the backboard, then dropped through the net without even touching the rim.

"Way to go!" Elizabeth said, clapping.

Bruce scowled at her.

Jessica ran to get the ball, then passed it smoothly

to Todd. He took his position, aimed, and shot. He made it. Aaron made it, and Bruce made it, but Rick missed.

"H," Bruce told him, and he nodded.

The next shot was a layup. Jessica made it, but Aaron got an H, and Rick got an O. On their foul-line shots, Jessica made it, and so did Aaron, Rick, and Bruce, but Todd got an H. Every time Jessica made a basket, Elizabeth, Maria, Amy, and Julie cheered.

Bruce grit his teeth. Why did he have to listen to this? What was worse, more of Jessica's airhead friends came over to watch, and soon there was a whole bevy of nosy females standing around and squealing like pigs every time Jessica made a basket. Bruce began to wish he had just stayed home and played tennis on his parents' court.

Bruce watched sourly as Jessica made a three-point shot. She ran up, caught the ball on the rebound, and passed it to her evil twin. Elizabeth looked surprised, then smiled. She ran to the front of the line and aimed carefully for her own three-point line shot. She made it.

Bruce groaned and slapped his palm against his forehead. What was America coming to if, without warning, a perfectly good game of Horse could be overrun by pesky females?

Fifteen minutes later, Rick, Todd, and Aaron were out. Jessica still had only an H, Elizabeth had an H-O, Janet had nothing, Lila was already out, and Maria had an H-O, too. Bruce had H-O-R-S. It was time for a snowball.

Trotting to the side of the court, he leaned down and picked up his T-shirt. "I gotta go, kids," he said, trying not to sound as out of breath as he felt. He used his T-shirt to wipe the sweat off his face, then put on his sunglasses.

"Yeah, OK," Jessica said absently, looking at the ball intently.

Bruce watched as the girls started playing a fast pickup game, with Elizabeth, Maria, Amy, Ellen, Julie, and Janet on one team, and Jessica, Lila, Belinda, Mandy, and Tamara on the other. They didn't even notice when Bruce left the court and got on his bicycle. The other guys had already left. As Bruce pedaled off toward his house, he could hear the girls cheering each other and giggling and squealing when they made points. It was disgusting, he thought darkly. Why couldn't girls stay on the sidelines, cheerleading, where they belonged?

Jessica could feel her heart pounding with excitement as Janet grabbed the ball out of Maria's hands. Janet dribbled twice, faked to the left, and threw the ball to Elizabeth.

Catching the ball, Elizabeth ran with her team in a fast break down the court. Almost immediately Jessica pounded up behind her in an aggressive guarding stance. Sweat dripped down her temple, and she brushed it away with one hand. She tried to block her sister, but Elizabeth leaped up and made a successful layup shot.

"All right!" Amy cheered, slapping her a high

five. The ball bounced from the rebound, and Maria scooped it up.

"Good one, Lizzie," Jessica said, panting.

"Gosh, what time is it?" Maria asked, tucking a stray strand of dark, curly hair back in her ponytail.

"Oh, wow, it's getting dark," Elizabeth said.

Jessica looked around. Sure enough, the park was practically deserted.

"Hey, when did the guys leave?" Amy asked, sitting down on the grass by the court. "I didn't even notice."

"Me neither." Jessica grinned. "But I did notice that we were playing fabulous basketball."

"You said it," Janet agreed, wiping her face on her tank top.

"It was a lot more fun than when we play basketball in gym," Lila said, gathering up her towel and beach bag. "Even though I totally ruined my nail polish."

One by one, the girls gathered their things, and Elizabeth, Maria, and Amy put their Rollerblades back on. As a group, the girls headed toward the park exit.

"No wonder the boys are always playing," Tamara said, swinging her tote by her side. "It really was fun. Even though we got all yucky and hot."

"Too bad we don't have an official girls' basketball team at school," Belinda added. "Just the boys'."

Suddenly a lightbulb went off in Jessica's head. She stopped dead in her tracks. "Why don't we?" In her mind's eye, she could already see herself in an official uniform, running onto a basketball court. "We could start the very first all-girl basketball team at SVMS!"

Elizabeth's eyes lit up. "That's a great idea, Jess," she said excitedly. "They have to let us. If the boys have a team, it would be sexist not to let us have a team, too."

"You're right," Amy agreed happily. "Man, playing on our own team would be so awesome!"

Tamara frowned. "Aren't you guys forgetting something? Basketball season's practically over."

Lila nodded. "And we use all of our spare time practicing for the Boosters."

"Boosters, schmoosters!" Jessica exclaimed. "We know all those routines by heart. And so what if the season's almost over? Are you telling me that no one here has ever *not* bought a new bathing suit because *summer* was almost over?"

"Don't be ridiculous," Lila said, tossing her hair. "Why should a little thing like *that* keep me from buying a suit?"

Tamara smiled a little. "Yeah, I guess I see your point."

"OK, then," Jessica said. "Let's vote. Who wants to start the first all-girl basketball team at SVMS?"

Eleven voices yelled aye, clear and loud.

"So it's set," Jessica said triumphantly. "As of tomorrow, we're a team!"

Three

"I'm sorry, girls," Coach Cassels said on Monday afternoon. "I wish you had come to me at the beginning of the school year. We definitely could have worked something out. But now it's just too late."

"Too late?" Jessica echoed. "What do you mean?"

"Basketball season is almost over," the coach said. "It won't be that long till we start the regional championships."

"We know that," Elizabeth broke in. "But there's nothing in the rules that says we have to play a whole season to get to the regionals. If we get started now, we still have enough time. But we need a coach, and we need to practice."

Coach Cassels shook his head again. "I'm sorry. But neither Assistant Coach Brimley nor I have any spare time to take on another after-school coaching obligation."

"Well, we'll just coach ourselves then," Jessica declared.

"There's one other problem," Coach Cassels said. "I'm afraid the gym courts are reserved for the boys' basketball team. We didn't schedule for them to share the use of the courts with another team. If we had known that there was going to be a girls' team . . ."

"Fine," Amy said, tucking a basketball firmly under her arm. "We'll just use the outside courts."

"I admire your determination, girls." Coach Cassels smiled. "And I really wish I could be of more help. There's just one last thing. You have to petition the local league to start up a new team."

"What?" Maria cried. "What kind of petition?"

"It just means that you have to write a formal letter of intent to the board members of the local league organization," he explained. "Tell them you're starting your team, the team's name, your school, and so forth. Once they approve the formation of your team, they'll start scheduling games with other schools. It shouldn't take too long. There's a registration fee of forty-five dollars. Good luck, girls." Coach Cassels smiled once more and headed across the gym to his office.

Jessica sighed, looking after him. This was turning out to be much more complicated than she had expected.

"Ugh," Belinda said, looking discouraged. "Maybe this wasn't such a good idea, guys."

Jessica set her jaw. "It *was* a good idea," she insisted. "It still is. So what if we're having a few setbacks? We just have to find ways around them."

"Well, Amy and I could handle the petition," Maria offered. "We can write the letter and everything. But where are we going to get the money for registration?"

"Maybe we could all chip in our allowances," Jessica suggested. "Or we could ask kids around school to sponsor us."

Tamara looked uncomfortable. "Wow, this seems like a lot of work."

Janet nodded. "Forming a basketball team was one thing." She sniffed. "Going around asking people for donations is another."

"But—" Jessica broke off, biting her lip. She had to admit, she wasn't crazy about registering or scrambling to collect money, either. And a few days ago, she couldn't have cared less about playing basketball. In fact, she thought of it as just a sweaty, yucky sport. She hadn't realized till now how exciting playing could be. Sure, being a Booster was great, but she was tired of cheering on the sidelines. She wanted to be in the center of the action.

She stared intently at the Unicorns. "So that's it? You guys are totally wimping out?"

Janet folded her arms. "We're just trying to be practical, Jessica. And there's no getting around the fact that basketball is a totally sweaty sport."

"And the uniforms aren't even that cute," Lila added. "Tennis outfits are much cuter."

"I can't believe you guys!" Jessica cried, even though she wasn't too wild about the uniforms herself. "I mean, do you just want to kick around on the sidelines while the boys steal the show?"

Janet frowned. "I hardly think—"

"Do you want to be the ones only doing the cheering," Jessica went on, "instead of the ones being cheered? Do you want to always be in the supporting role?"

A shadow seemed to pass over Janet's face. "Supporting role?"

Lila bit her lip, and the other Unicorns looked at their feet. Jessica and Elizabeth exchanged glances.

"Well, maybe we could wear really cute uniforms," Janet suggested. "Something different. Not just tank tops and shorts."

Lila brightened a little. "That's so *done.* But with adorable uniforms, we might not make such a bad team."

Jessica let out her breath. She *knew* she could make the Unicorns see the light.

"Do you really think we can coach ourselves?" Julie Porter asked a few moments later. The girls were sitting on the bleachers, planning their next move.

"Sure we can," Jessica said firmly. "Why not?"

"Maybe Janet should be the coach," Lila said. "After all, she *is* the president of the Unicorns."

"And she knows absolutely diddly about basketball," Jessica pointed out.

"Hey! Wait a minute!" Janet said, her hands on her hips.

Jessica realized she had gone too far. "Umm, no offense, Janet," she said quickly. "You're a great player.

And you're a great Unicorn president. It's just that, well, in terms of coaching basketball . . . umm, well, your strengths seem to lie elsewhere, you know?"

Janet shrugged, still looking a bit disgruntled. "Fine. I don't really want to coach, anyway. I say we all sort of coach ourselves."

"Good idea," Jessica said, then turned to the rest of her teammates. "I think that covers all the bases. Let's set our first practice for day after tomorrow, since the Boosters have to cheer at the SVMS–Big Mesa game tomorrow afternoon."

"Gee, Steamin' Steven," the boy said. "Do you think maybe one day I'll be able to shoot like that?"

Steven smiled down at the sixth-grader. "Sure, kid. Just watch what I do, and try to imitate it." He dribbled the basketball down the court. The hard ball thumped loudly on the wooden floor. The gym was filled with the sounds of other kids practicing their skills. Gracefully Steven leaped up and dropped the ball through the hoop. When he looked back, the boy was gazing at him with admiration.

With a sigh, Steven shifted in his chair. After school he had stopped by the coach's office and picked up an application for the assistant coach position. Now he was at home, in the den, trying to fill it out.

The first part had been easy: name, address, school. Basketball experience, position played, stats, et cetera. But there were also some essay questions, and they were much harder.

Steven stared at the cake crumbs on his plate. He'd figured that some chocolate cake would help him think, but already he'd had two large pieces, and he was still stuck. He stared down at the first essay question.

"What are the most important things to teach young basketball players?"

Steven chewed on his pen cap. Most important? That was hard. Everything was important: you had to know how to shoot, how to run, how to pass, how to play both offense and defense, how to set up shots for other players . . . it was hard to pick one thing.

Steven took a sip of milk, and then it hit him. The application had been written by a grown-up: They wanted him to write about good sportsmanship, teamwork, and stuff like that.

"I think the most important things to teach young basketball players is that winning isn't as important as playing your best, and that sincere effort and teamwork matter more than how many points an individual scores."

Steven sat back, a pleased smile on his face. Grown-ups loved this kind of stuff. He bet the coach would eat it up.

He went on to question number two.

"We need to come up with a cool name." Jessica's voice broke into Steven's thoughts. He turned in irritation as his sisters burst into the den from the kitchen. Jessica flung her backpack down onto the couch, then flopped dramatically beside it.

"Yeah," Elizabeth said, setting down her own backpack neatly by the door. "We can come up with some suggestions, and then vote on them at our next practice."

Steven sighed to himself. *The Invasion of the Pointless Sisters.* "Kids, I'm trying to work here," he growled.

Jessica gasped and pressed her hand to her forehead. "Steven Wakefield, doing homework *before* dinner? Oh, my gosh, I think I might faint."

"Hardy de hardy har har," Steven said dryly. "Seriously, take a hike, you guys. I have to concentrate."

"What are you working on?" Elizabeth asked, coming to look over his shoulder.

Steven let out his breath. What was he expecting? Of course a guy couldn't have privacy in this house. That would be too much to ask. Of course a guy couldn't just sit quietly and work on the most important job application of his life without a couple of pests bothering him and making noise and butting into his business, could he? No, of course not.

"It's an application for the assistant coach position at the basketball summer camp," he explained. "And I'm trying to fill it out. So go away."

"Can't," Jessica said flatly, reaching for the TV remote. "It's time for *Lifestyles of the French and Famous.* Which you know is my favorite show, right after *Days of Turmoil.*"

Steven groaned. "Don't make me watch that stupid show," he complained. "I have to answer some very important essay questions about basketball. How can I concentrate with that idiot Chef Crepe babbling in the background?"

"Go to your room to work," Jessica said unsympathetically, her eyes on the TV. "There's something there that will help you a lot."

"Oh, yeah? What's that?"

"A desk." Jessica looked at Elizabeth, and they both dissolved into giggles.

"I hate little sisters," Steven murmured under his breath, gathering up his application and his pen.

"What did you say?" Elizabeth asked, curling up on the couch next to Jessica.

"Nothing." Sighing, Steven pushed his chair back, making as much noise as possible. Then he clattered his plate and glass together, trying to irritate Jessica.

"Shhh!" Jessica said impatiently, waving her hand.

Steven put on a long-suffering face. "I guess there's no way you two would understand," he said sadly. "You're just *girls.* I'm trying to plan my future in a manly, demanding sport, but you're still all wrapped up in what Malibu Barbie is going to wear to the prom."

"Steven," Elizabeth said in a pained voice, "you know good and well that we haven't played with Barbies for ages."

"Yeah, whatever you say," Steven replied, making his way to the door.

"And for your information," Elizabeth added, "you're looking at two of the members of the first all-girl team of that manly, demanding sport at Sweet Valley Middle School."

"What?" Steven paused and turned around. Jessica unglued her eyes from the screen for a minute and nodded proudly.

"Yep," Elizabeth said. "We still have to come up with a name and uniforms, but as soon as the league board members give their approval, we'll be an official basketball team."

Steven stared at them. "You're kidding. Why in the world are you guys doing that? You don't even like basketball."

"We just didn't realize how much we liked it," Jessica clarified. "But we do. And we're really good."

"Oh, come on." Steven leaned against the door frame. "How good could you be? I mean, it's pretty hard to play basketball without smearing your mascara."

Elizabeth's eyes narrowed. "Sexist pig."

"Yeah," Jessica agreed, her eyes on the TV screen. "Sexist pig."

Steven decided to ignore that comment. "Well, tell me this. If you're a real team, who's your coach?"

"Actually," Elizabeth admitted, "we don't have an actual coach. But we're having our first practice on Wednesday. Want to come check us out?"

"Yeah, right." Steven laughed disbelievingly. "Like I'm really tempted to come watch a bunch of sixth-grade girls play basketball."

"Not all of us are in sixth grade," Elizabeth told him. "Anyway, we'll be at the outdoor court at school if you change your mind."

Steven smirked. "Don't hold your breath."

Four

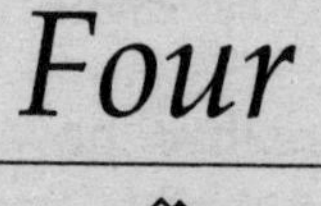

"Lean to the left!
"Lean to the right!
"Come on, guys,
"Fight, fight, fight!
"Yay, Wolverines!"

"Wow, look at the Boosters," Julie Porter said. She and Elizabeth were covering the Tuesday afternoon SVMS–Big Mesa game for the *Sixers*. "They're really whipping the crowd into a frenzy. Hold on—let me write that down."

Elizabeth nodded, her eyes on the fast-paced game. Todd was pounding down the court, dribbling the ball expertly. He passed the ball to Bruce, who passed it to Aaron, who scored two points with a great jump shot.

"All right!" Elizabeth shouted, leaping up and

punching her fist in the air. Next to her, Maria Slater and Sophia Rizzo were clapping and stomping their feet on the wooden stands.

"Man, if the Wolverines win this game, it'll be their sixth win in a row," Sophia said excitedly. She also worked on the *Sixers.*

Just then Bruce made a great layup shot while Ken Matthews defended him, and the Wolverines were six points ahead.

"Go, Wolverines!" Maria shouted, clapping loudly.

On the sidelines, the Boosters did a grapevine to the left, then one to the right. Their short pleated skirts fanned out around them, and their pom-poms shook at high speed.

"Give me a W!
"Give me an O!
"Give me an L!"

As the Boosters spelled out "Wolverines," Elizabeth joined the rest of the SVMS fans, yelling out the letters, too. Then a huge wave started at one end of their bleachers and rolled through the crowd.

"I know that as a journalist, I'm supposed to be keeping an unbiased mind," Sophia said breathlessly once they had all sat down again. "But I'm so excited I can hardly sit still to take notes!"

Elizabeth nodded. "I know what you mean. The Wolverines are playing an amazing game—of course we're going to get all caught up in it."

"Maybe we should start doing player profiles," Julie suggested. "Feature a different Wolverine each week and interview them."

"That's a great idea, Julie," Elizabeth said. She bit her lip when the Wolverines suddenly cut down the court in a fast break. Tim Davis shot the ball to Bruce, who made one last basket just as the final buzzer sounded.

"Yay!" Elizabeth, Maria, Sophia, and Julie shouted. "Way to go, Wolverines!" All around them, the Sweet Valley Middle School crowd erupted into screams of victory.

On the court, the team members were slapping each other high fives and jumping up and down. Coach Cassels was waving his hat in the air. The Big Mesa fans were either booing glumly or filing silently out of the gym.

The Boosters were doing split jumps, and Grace Oliver had leaped onto Winston Egbert's shoulders.

"Six games in a row!" the Boosters cheered.
"You can't beat Wolverines!
"Six games in a row!
"The best you've ever seen! Yay!"

The Boosters did high kicks, then instantly dropped into position for their famous six-person pyramid. When Jessica took her place on the very top, the SVMS crowd cheered louder than ever.

"The Boosters are fantastic," Sophia said,

scribbling quickly in her notebook. "They get better all the time."

"They really help get the crowd into it," Elizabeth agreed.

Maria tapped her feet restlessly. "Seeing this is getting me so psyched to start playing on *our* team."

"Me too," Julie reminded. "It'll be so much fun to have everyone come to our games and stuff."

Elizabeth gazed at the celebration on the court and on the stands all around her. She felt an incredible wave of excitement herself. "Tomorrow's our first practice," she reminded them. "It won't be long before everyone's cheering our names!"

"Unicorn All-Stars! No way!" Amy cried, looking at Tamara in disbelief.

"It's the perfect name," Janet argued. "After all, most of us *are* Unicorns."

Jessica grinned. Janet did have a point there.

"But not all of us," Elizabeth pointed out impatiently. She looked at her watch. "So far we've wasted half an hour trying to pick a name. We haven't shot even one basket yet!"

"We need a team name for our petition," Maria reminded her. "So we better pick one soon."

"Let's go around in a circle and each person suggest one name," Elizabeth said. She reached into her backpack and pulled out her notebook. "Then we'll vote."

"How about the Girl Wolverines?" Belinda suggested.

"Ugh," Amy commented.

"What kind of team name is Ugh?" Ellen demanded.

"Ha ha," Amy said dryly. "My suggestion is the Amazons. The Sweet Valley Middle School Amazons."

Jessica sighed. What they needed was something really cute and catchy. A name that said something about them as a team.

Ellen snapped her fingers. "I say we should be the SVMS Bachelorettes."

"Bachelorettes?" Janet repeated. "Ellen, this isn't a dating show."

"How about the Warriors?" Maria asked. "There's no reason why we have to have a girly name. Let's show them we mean business."

"The Peaches," Lila chimed in. "That's cute and feminine."

"Yeah, and real athletic." Jessica smirked. "We'd scare every team off the court with that name."

"And I suppose you have something better?" Lila retorted.

"It's not my turn yet!" Jessica defended herself. She hugged her knees to her chest, racking her brain. All the best teams had great nicknames—even some of the best athletes. Like Air Jordan, Jessica thought. Or was that a sneaker? Whatever. And what had Muhammad Ali said, back when Jessica's parents were in college? "Float like a butterfly, sting like a . . ."

"I like the Warriors," Mandy said, smiling at Maria.

"Umm, maybe the SVMS Magic?" Julie suggested. "Like the pro team?"

"The Honeybees!" Jessica blurted out. "We can be the Honeybees."

Elizabeth smiled. "Hey, that's kind of cute."

"Well, it's not your turn yet, Jessica," Lila informed her. "It's *Janet's* turn, in fact."

Janet was frowning in concentration. "The Honeybees," she murmured. "You know, it has kind of a nice ring to it. It says cute, fast, sweet . . ."

"It says fuzzy, flying insect with a stinger on its rear," Lila objected.

From the smiles on her teammates' faces—all her teammates but Lila, anyway—Jessica knew the vote was clinched. "All in favor of Honeybees?" she asked. Hands raised, and Elizabeth quickly counted them.

"Majority vote!" she said happily. "The Honeybees it is! Now let's get to work."

"This isn't working!" Jessica called out an hour later.

"What's wrong?" Tamara asked, brushing her hair out of her eyes.

"We need to all do the same thing at the same time! We can't have Mandy running laps and Elizabeth shooting baskets and Ellen doing jumping jacks. It's a total mess!" Jessica exploded. "We need to work together as a team!"

"You said we could each choose what we wanted to do," Ellen reminded her.

"I was wrong, OK?" Jessica crossed her arms over her chest.

"Jessica's right," Maria said. "Other teams work

out together. How are we supposed to mesh as a team if we don't?"

"Fine, then," Lila said. "Let's start with some aerobic warm-ups."

"I think we should build stamina by running laps," Amy protested.

"The boys' team does push-ups and sit-ups," Julie put in.

"Actually, I know what we should do," Lila said decisively.

Jessica looked at her skeptically. "What's that?"

Lila pointed to the sky as a light, chilly drizzle began to fall. "Go home!"

"We can't," Jessica argued. "We still have an hour of practice left."

"But it's gross outside," Belinda complained, rubbing her arms with her hands to warm up.

Jessica was considering doing something drastic with the basketball when Elizabeth stepped in.

"Are you guys going to just give up?" Elizabeth pushed her wet bangs off her forehead. "Do you think the boys would give up just because of a little rain?"

"No, they wouldn't," Janet snapped. "And do you know why?" She didn't wait for an answer. "Because they're practicing *inside* in the *warm, well-lit gym*!"

Jessica bit her lip. As much as she wanted to get their team into shape, she had to admit that Janet had a point. So far, their practice was a total mess, and as far as she could tell, it wasn't going to get any better. The cold rain raised goosebumps on her arms. She was starting to feel chilly and clammy herself.

"You know what the problem is?" Elizabeth asked quietly. "The problem is that we really do need a coach—one coach. If we had someone who was on our side, who wanted to help shape us into a team, someone who knew what he—or she—was doing, none of us would feel this bad."

For a few moments, Jessica and the rest of the Honeybees were silent. Then Jessica took a deep breath.

"You're right, Lizzie," she said. "We need one person to take charge—one person we'll all listen to."

"But who?" Belinda wailed. "None of the school coaches will help us."

"We could hire a coach," Maria said doubtfully.

"With what money?" Tamara asked. "It's taking all our resources just to come up with the registration fee—and we haven't even talked about uniforms yet."

Janet sighed. "Oh, I saw the cutest uniforms at Gaynor's sporting goods shop."

Mandy giggled. "She means she saw the cutest Steven Wakefield standing next to some uniforms at Gaynor's sporting goods shop."

Jessica rolled her eyes. "First things first. Uniforms and Steven have nothing to do with—hey, that's it!"

"What's it?" Julie asked.

"Steven!" Jessica said triumphantly. "He might be

a total pain—in fact, he *is* a total pain—but he's a good coach. I know he is."

"Steven?" Elizabeth asked, her eyes wide.

"Yeah . . . Steven," Janet said thoughtfully, her cheeks turning pink. "That's a good idea. I mean, he *is* a really great player."

Jessica smirked to herself. She knew at least *one* person who would vote for him!

"I don't know." Lila sniffed. "Steven can be a drag sometimes."

"I'm not sure about this idea," Elizabeth said, "but we don't really have a lot of options right now. Why don't we give him a probation period, like a week or two weeks? If we don't think he's doing a good job, we can fire him."

"That's a good idea," Maria said, nodding.

"Yeah—what could it hurt to try? Nothing could get worse than this practice," Amy agreed.

"Let's take a vote," Jessica said quickly. "All in favor?"

The ayes had it, and Jessica grinned in satisfaction. Now all she had to do was convince Steven.

Five

"Are you out of your cotton-pickin' mind?" Steven bellowed that night after dinner.

"But you *like* to coach, remember?" Jessica argued. "And we really need help. Come on—you don't want your sisters to humiliate themselves, do you?"

"Yeah, like I care," Steven scoffed. "There is no way I'm spending my afternoons trying to get a bunch of wimpy girls to play a decent game of basketball."

"Steven, for your information, we are *not* wimpy girls," Elizabeth said angrily. "In fact, we're already pretty good. We just need a little guidance."

"Get a coach from school." Steven sat down at his desk and pulled out his earth sciences textbook.

"We've tried!" Jessica said. "None of them will help us. They're all already busy."

"Well, so am I," Steven said, studying a page in his book. "Include me out."

"Steven!" Elizabeth said, sending Jessica a frustrated look. "Can't you help us just this once? Please?"

"Sorry, kid," Steven said briskly, not even looking up. "No can do."

"Steven," Jessica began humbly. "Please. I'm asking you, as your younger sister, to help us with our basketball team."

"You should have thought of that before you pushed me in the pool, blondie," Steven said, tapping his pencil against his cheek.

"Arrggh!" Jessica growled in exasperation. "Let's get out of here, Lizzie!"

She stomped out of Steven's room, Elizabeth at her heels.

Today's the day, Steven thought as he headed through the halls of Sweet Valley High to Coach Berger's office on Thursday afternoon. He had been working on his application all week and had finally turned it in this morning. During lunch, he had gotten a message to meet Coach Berger after school for an interview.

When Steven arrived at the small, glassed-in office off the gym, there were already eight other guys waiting. Most of them were older than Steven, and several of them were senior varsity. But Steven wasn't worried. He knew he was perfect for this job. His application had been killer.

One by one, the applicants filed inside for their interviews. One by one, they filed out. Steven noticed that several of them looked pleased and relaxed when they came out. Maybe the coach had let them down easy.

Finally it was his turn, and Coach Berger came to the door, looking down at his clipboard. "Steven Wakefield?"

Steven got up and followed the coach into his office. The office was small and painted white and smelled kind of plasticky. Steven sat down in a beat-up chair across from the coach's desk.

"Steven," Coach Berger said, "you had a very good application. You're a good basketball player yourself, and I really liked your answers on the essay questions."

Steven smiled. "Oh, thanks, Coach," he said offhandedly. *I am in, baby.*

"But I have to turn you down for the assistant coach position at the basketball camp this summer."

Steven felt his eyes widen and his mouth drop open a little bit. He shut it with a snap. Maybe there was some mistake. Maybe he had misheard. "Excuse me?" he asked, waiting to hear the coach say he was just kidding.

"You have no coaching experience," Coach Berger said bluntly. "I need someone who's experienced in working with kids this age. I need to know that you can handle the job—that you have practical experience in all aspects of coaching. I need someone who knows the ropes. I won't have time to be showing you how to handle the kids."

"But . . . but I thought you liked my application," Steven stammered.

"I did," Coach Berger said. "But you just don't have enough experience. Sorry."

"But how am I supposed to get experience if you won't hire me?" Steven asked desperately.

Coach Berger shrugged sympathetically. "That's always the problem," he said, "and I don't have the answer. I'm sorry, Steven. Your application was really good. If you had experience, I'd hire you in a second. But I just can't."

Steven sat there for a moment, paralyzed by disappointment. He'd been counting on this job. Not only did he want the extra money, but he had to think about his long-term plans. After his fantastic pro career in the NBA petered out, coaching would be the best way for him to keep involved in basketball. Now, just because Coach Berger wouldn't give him experience, all those plans were falling apart.

Looking up, he saw that Coach Berger was obviously waiting for him to leave. "Well, thanks anyway," he said, standing quickly. He held out his hand and shook the coach's. Just as he was leaving, an idea suddenly came to him. "Say, Coach," he said. "If I somehow got experience, like, by coaching kids that age, would you reconsider?"

Coach Berger stroked his mustache. "Yeah, I guess I would." His smile told Steven that he thought Steven had about as much chance as a cold day in July. In California. "Not all of the positions have been filled," the coach added. "But I don't see how you can get experience in the next couple of weeks."

Steven felt a smile creep onto his face. "Oh, I'll try to come up with something. Thanks, Coach. Thanks a lot!"

"This came awfully quick," Janet muttered as she laced her sneakers tightly on Saturday morning.

"Tell me about it," Lila moaned.

"We just have to do our best," Elizabeth said firmly, braiding her long hair to keep it out of her face. "It may only be our first game, but it won't be our last. Let's go out there and show them we mean business."

Maria stood in front of a mirror in the Palisades girls' locker room. Her pretty face looked worried, and she was chewing nervously on her lip. "I can't believe we're playing our first game only one day after our petition was approved."

Mandy nodded as she tugged her T-shirt down. "Especially since we've had only two practices."

"And they were both lousy." Belinda fastened her knee guards and stood up.

"We're going to get creamed," Julie said soberly.

Elizabeth sighed. She was feeling pretty uncertain herself, but she didn't think this defeatist attitude was going to get them anywhere. "We'll just have to go out there and do our best. I'm sure we'll be great," she said as optimistically as possible. She glanced around at her teammates. They all looked like lambs going to the slaughter. "Let's go out there and show them the Honeybees are here to stay."

* * *

"Maybe the Honeybees aren't actually here to stay after all," Elizabeth muttered under her breath at the end of the first half. Palisades' cheerleaders were on the court, performing their brief halftime show. Wearing little black cat costumes, the cheerleaders were bouncing around the entire court, yelling about how fabulous the Palisades Pantherettes were.

"I hate them," Lila said in a low tone from where she was sitting on the bench. "And their costumes are totally yesterday." She took a white towel and wiped her forehead.

"This was a big mistake," Janet said, gulping down a sports drink.

"Why do you say that?" Ellen asked snippily. "Just because they're leading twenty-four to two, it doesn't mean anything."

"It *is* pretty depressing," Elizabeth admitted softly from where she sat next to Jessica.

"Yeah, but look at them," Jessica said irritably. Her face was flushed and damp, and she pulled her T-shirt away from her body to fan it. "Their side of the bleachers is packed with fans. Look at our side."

Elizabeth glanced behind them. Their bleachers were completely empty, even though she had advertised their game in the *Sixers* and Maria had put up posters all around school.

"They have cheerleaders," Jessica continued, morosely watching them. "We have nobody. They have a coach." She gestured toward the Pantherettes' coach, who was striding up and down the side court, patting her players reassuringly on their backs. "We don't have a coach."

Just then the halftime whistle blew, and with a collective groan, the Honeybees got to their feet and straggled onto the court.

Might as well get this over with, Elizabeth thought. *Might as well just let the Pantherettes cream us so we can all go take nice, cool showers.*

In the end, the score was a totally mortifying thirty-eight to six. Feeling like a piece of gum someone had spit onto the sidewalk, Jessica collapsed on their bench and buried her face in her towel. This had been one of the worst days of her life.

As the triumphant Palisades Pantherettes were cheered by their fans, coach, and cheerleaders, the rest of the humiliated Honeybees slunk together in a defeated circle and left the court, not even meeting each other's eyes.

Jessica felt Elizabeth plop down next to her, then the bench rattled as, one by one, the Honeybees parked themselves. Across the court, the Pantherettes were being carried out of the gym on the shoulders of their ecstatic fans. Cheers, hoots, and whistles filled the air and rang in Jessica's ears. She kept her face buried in her towel. She couldn't bear to see the Pantherettes—and she couldn't face her teammates, either.

"Well, it was only a game," Elizabeth murmured.

"Yeah," Lila said tiredly. "And the QE2 is only a boat."

"So much for the first and the last game of the famous Honeybees," Janet said in disgust.

Earlier Jessica would have jumped up and rallied her team. Earlier she would have given them a pep talk, tried to buck them up, tried to convince them that they would be great. Now she just wanted to take a shower, go home, and crawl into bed. With any luck at all, her parents would never make her go back to school again. By Monday, everyone at SVMS would have heard about their monumental defeat. She couldn't face the humiliation.

Slowly the sounds of the Palisades contingent faded away—all except for one sound. It was the sound of one person clapping.

Taking the towel from her face, Jessica looked up warily. She saw the rest of the Honeybees look up at the same time. Across from them, sitting in the bleachers that the Palisades fans had just left, was Steven. He was clapping.

"Very funny, Steven," Jessica said in irritation. "Look, just go away, OK? We're not in the mood."

"I don't blame you," Steven said, stepping down the bleachers as if they were giant stairs. "After that game, I would just want to go home and hide. Boy, do you guys stink."

"Steven!" Elizabeth's eyes were narrow and angry. "How can you be so mean? Can't you tell how upset we are?"

Steven crossed the court to their side and stood with one foot up on their bench. "Let me finish," he said. "Of course you guys stink—it was your first game, you've been a team for less than a week, you don't have a coach, and you've had only two lousy practices. It would be amazing if you *had* managed to play well. I mean, it would have been a miracle. I mean, people would be lining up to worship at this gym, you know?"

"We get the picture, Steven," Lila snarled, crossing her arms over her chest. "What do you want?"

"I want to make you a proposition," Steven said. "It's true, you guys played awful. But it's also true that I saw some actual potential here. Janet, you're great at long passes, and you've got great hands."

"I do?" Janet blushed and looked pleased. "Gee, thanks, Steven. It's nice of you to notice." She tucked a strand of hair behind her ear.

Oh, brother, Jessica thought.

"Jessica," Steven said, "you've got a great outside shot. Elizabeth almost never misses her layups. Lila is actually a good point guard. And Maria played mean defense. It was like you'd all been taken over by pod people. Pod people who were decent players."

"Yeah? So?" Elizabeth asked warily.

Steven paced up and down. "So I'm saying your main problem is that you're totally disorganized." He thumped his fist into his palm. "You guys never play several moves ahead—you just rush in and flail around. You're not coordinated as a team. On my team, we try to move like one, smooth, integrated unit. Understand?"

Jessica saw Mandy and Amy nodding. The other

Honeybees were looking at their shoes. They couldn't deny it.

"Well, thanks for your observations, Steven," Jessica said breezily, standing up. "If that's all, we need to hit the showers."

"Hold your horses." Steven put up his hand, and Jessica reluctantly sat down. "As I said, I have a proposition."

"Well?" Maria prompted him.

"As it turns out," Steven began casually, "I happen to have a little free time over the next few weeks. I thought, if you guys are interested in keeping your team going, that I could spare some afternoons and coach you."

"What?" Jessica's mouth dropped open. "You said no way! You laughed at us! You said you'd rather die than—"

"OK, OK," Steven said testily. "I know what I said. I've changed my mind, OK? Now I find I have time. Are you interested or not?"

Jessica felt torn for a moment. On the one hand, she wanted to tell Steven to take a hike. After all, he had been totally obnoxious when she'd asked him to coach. On the other hand, this was probably the Honeybees' only hope, their only chance at having a coach at all.

"Just a second, Steven," she said. "We need a moment to talk about it."

Steven shrugged and moved a few feet away.

"What do you guys think?" Jessica asked her teammates in a low voice.

"I say we forget it," Lila said firmly. "I mean, if he had the nerve to turn us down once—"

"Well, I don't see why we have to hold a grudge," Janet broke in. "Steven is an incredible player, and I'm sure he'd make an incredible coach." She sighed dreamily. "We'd have to work closely with him, day in, day out . . ."

Ellen giggled, slapping her hand over her mouth.

Janet shot her a look, then cleared her throat. "I mean, you heard him. He thinks we have potential."

"Janet's right," Elizabeth said. "We *do* have potential, and we need a coach who will help us develop it."

"Yeah," Amy agreed. "And maybe Steven's that coach."

"He's the only one volunteering for the job," Mandy added, shrugging.

Jessica nodded. She still hated the idea of giving her brother any satisfaction, but she had to face it. They were desperate.

"All right!" Steven boomed. "Practice begins tomorrow morning. At eight thirty. Sharp."

"Eight thirty!" Lila cried. "On a Sunday? Are you insane?"

Steven put his hands on his hips and gave Lila a stern look. "No, I'm not insane," he said calmly. "I'm your coach. If I say eight thirty, I mean eight thirty. Anyone who's not there is off the team. We have a lot of catching up to do, and we have to get started now. Understand?"

"Oh, yes, Steven," Janet breathed.

Jessica nodded despite herself. Her brother was a worm, but he was a tough and professional-looking worm.

"And another thing," Steven said briskly. "I want everyone in a white T-shirt and gray gym shorts. No red, no purple, no patterns. White and gray. Got it?"

Mandy wrinkled her nose. "Why?"

"Because you've got to start thinking as a unit, a team. One way to get into that mindset is for all of you to look more or less the same. Any other questions?" Steven's brown eyes looked the team over.

Jessica tried to think of something that would annoy her brother, but somehow she couldn't. *Thinking as a team,* she repeated to herself, feeling a wave of excitement. *Maybe there's hope after all.*

Six

"Oh, my gosh," Maria gasped, pounding up next to Elizabeth on the outdoor track. "I . . . had . . . no . . . idea . . . how out of shape I was. I think I'm going to die."

Elizabeth nodded, pumping her arms and vaguely wondering if she could make it to the starting point before she keeled over. Steven had already made them run around the track three times, and now her calves were burning, her feet felt as if they each weighed twenty pounds, and her white T-shirt was clinging wetly to her back.

Just ahead she saw Steven standing at the starting point. He was holding a clipboard and a stopwatch. Janet staggered over the line, pausing only to smile limply at Steven. Jessica was next. Elizabeth and Maria plodded over the line, and they immediately collapsed on the grass by the side of the track, where gradually the rest of the Honeybees joined them.

"I hate this," Belinda wheezed.

Steven strolled up, holding his clipboard. He took his pencil from behind his ear and made a couple of notations. "OK. We'll have to work on your speed and stamina, obviously." He tucked the clipboard under one arm and clapped twice. "Now, I want two rows, one with six, one with five. Do it!"

Groaning, Elizabeth struggled to her feet. She fell into line with her teammates, who all looked as bedraggled and wiped out as she felt.

"Give me some jumping jacks," Steven commanded, and clapped twice again.

It must be almost time for lunch, Elizabeth thought, jumping weakly. *No wonder I'm so beat.*

When Steven blew his whistle, she quickly glanced at her watch. It said nine fifteen. *Only nine fifteen?* she thought, shaking her watch. *It has to be broken.*

"OK, on the ground!" Steven blew his whistle again. "We're doing stomach crunches."

Elizabeth dropped to the ground next to Julie. "I'm going to shove that whistle down his throat in a minute," she whispered. "What time do you have?"

"Nine seventeen," Julie whispered back.

Elizabeth groaned.

Steven looked at her pointedly. "Ms. Wakefield, do you have a problem?"

"No, no problem," Elizabeth replied through gritted teeth.

* * *

"I feel like we've been here forever," Janet moaned an hour later. She glanced at Steven, who was standing near the basket. "But I'm OK," she added quickly.

"I feel like we're *going* to be here forever," Lila whimpered next to her in line.

Jessica knew how they felt. She didn't know what was worse: the horrible public humiliation of their defeat at the hands of the Palisades Pantherettes, or this grueling, unending workout at the hands of her sadistic brother.

The Honeybees, after an hour and a half of calisthenics, were now practicing jump shots, outside shots, long shots, and layups.

"Every muscle in my body feels like overcooked spaghetti," Mandy said dully as the line shuffled forward.

"I don't even want to think about how I'll feel tomorrow," Jessica said.

Tamara took her shot, caught the ball, then passed it to Jessica, who was next in line.

Steven, standing on the sidelines, clapped twice. "Let's look lively, ladies!" he called. "Just a few more rotations and you can hit the showers. You're doing great! Just keep it up."

"I'd like to keep it up," Amy muttered darkly. "I'd like to keep it up his nose."

"Ms. Sutton?" Steven said sharply. "Do you have a problem?"

Amy hung her head. "No, no problem," she muttered.

"Good." Steven clapped twice again.

"Does he have to keep clapping like that?" Jessica hissed to Tamara, once she'd taken her shot and passed the ball to Janet. "I feel like I'm supposed to roll over and play dead or something."

Tamara nodded. "I wouldn't mind playing dead right now. At least I'd be on the ground."

"Janet!" Steven called. "Take that shot over. And this time, visualize the ball going into the basket. Concentrate."

"Oh, OK, Steven." Janet beamed and wiped the sweat from her forehead as she trotted tiredly over to pick up the ball. "Thanks. I'll try harder."

Dreamily Elizabeth gazed up at the sky, her eyelids drooping. Practice had just ended, and she and the rest of the Honeybees were lying limply on the grass by the outdoor court.

"What are you going to do this afternoon?" Maria mumbled next to her. Her eyes were closed, her arms flat out by her sides.

"Ngh," Elizabeth managed to say.

"Me too," Maria said dully.

Nearby, Jessica stretched her arms halfheartedly before letting them drop to the ground. "How are you getting home, Lila?" she asked, her words slurred.

"Don't know," Lila answered weakly. "I brought my bike. But now I might call our gardener to come get me in the wheelbarrow."

"My mom's coming," Janet said from where she

was sprawled out. "You could have a ride."

"That would involve me getting up," Lila protested tiredly. "No way."

"Ladies, ladies," Steven said, walking up to them.

Elizabeth felt her stomach knot.

"Isn't practice over?" Mandy asked fearfully.

"I don't think I can do any more," Maria said, her voice cracking.

Elizabeth braced herself for the horrible sound of his whistle.

But Steven grinned at them, not whistling or clapping. "You all did great," he said, sounding peppy. "Much better than I expected."

"Oh, wonderful," Tamara groaned.

"It was a hard workout, but you all came through," Steven continued. "I'm proud of you."

Elizabeth opened her eyes. He was proud of them?

"The first time is always the hardest," Steven went on. "But next time it'll be easier, and it'll keep getting easier. I bet by next week, you're all going to be iron women."

"Iron women?" Maria giggled. "I like the sound of that."

"And you know what?" Steven said. Elizabeth, along with several of her teammates, sat up to listen. "I bet you're working harder than the Palisades Pantherettes or any other team in the league. And that'll make you better and stronger. After the season is over, and you guys are the regional champions, I bet the other teams will wish they had worked as hard and shown as much guts as you all have. They're going to feel like total wimps."

"Regional champions?" Tamara asked, her eyes wide. "Do you really think we have a shot?"

"Between your playing and my coaching, yes, I think you have a shot." Steven nodded firmly.

Elizabeth felt a surge of excitement. "You know, if we could really become regional champions, all this hard work just might be worth it." She glanced wryly at Maria. "That is, if Steven doesn't kill us first."

"Attitude, Wakefield," Steven growled at her.

Elizabeth giggled.

"The Pantherettes are wimps," Jessica said, fanning her face. "I bet we'll beat them next time."

"You definitely will," Steven said confidently. "Now hit the showers. I'll see you back here on Tuesday afternoon at three thirty."

"Pick those legs up!" Steven shouted through his megaphone.

"I hate him, I hate him, I hate him," Jessica muttered rhythmically as she trotted around the outdoor track. The hot Tuesday afternoon sun beat down on her head, and her long blond hair was already limp and damp.

Lila struggled to keep up with Jessica. "I have an idea," she panted. "Let's all gang up on Steven after practice and kill him."

"You got my vote," Jessica agreed as they rounded a corner.

"I know we're supposed to be turning into iron

women," Mandy complained as she pulled up alongside Jessica and Lila. "But I feel more like I'm turning into spaghetti woman."

"Tell me about it," Jessica puffed. "Yesterday when I woke up, I felt like I'd been rolled over by a tractor."

"I was just starting to recover," Ellen complained. "But now all my muscles are screaming in agony again."

"Oh, come on, you guys," Janet wheezed, flashing a smile at Steven across the track. "It's hard work, but Steven knows best. You don't want him to think you're sissies, do you?" She wiggled her fingers at Steven.

"I don't know, Janet," Lila huffed. "For those of us who don't have true love urging them on, this sort of torture doesn't seem worth it."

Jessica was about to agree, when she sensed someone pounding at her heels.

"Out of the way, girls!"

Jessica turned to see the Wolverines, running in military precision around the outside track. Quickly Jessica, Lila, and the other Honeybees clustered over on one side. The Wolverines, hardly looking at them, tromped by in perfect rows.

"Time to practice, time to run," Bruce yelled in an imitation marines chant.

"Time to practice, time to run," the Wolverines repeated in one voice.

"We're Wolverines, this is our fun," Bruce chanted as the Wolverines blew past the Honeybees.

"We're Wolverines, this is our fun," the team echoed.

"Hey, Aaron," Jessica panted as he plodded past with his team, but he wouldn't turn his head.

"Hi, Ken!" Amy called to her sort-of boyfriend. He didn't respond.

Elizabeth waved at Todd, her own sort-of boyfriend, but he didn't glance at her.

Eyes forward, shoulders back, legs pumping in perfect time, the boys' basketball team left the Honeybees in a cloud of dust.

"Don't say hi or anything!" Jessica yelled after Aaron angrily.

"Yeah," Amy shouted at Ken Matthews's back. "Hello to you, too!"

Leaving the team to continue jogging ahead, Bruce trotted back. "Quit bothering my athletes," he said severely, still running in place. "We've got an important practice going on. Unlike you, we plan to win our next game."

Jessica gasped. Who did he think he was, to rub their defeat in their faces?

Then, without a backward glance, Bruce turned and ran to catch up to the rest of the Wolverines.

For a few moments, Jessica just stood on the sidelines, her mouth open in shock. She looked at Lila, and Lila's dark eyes were flashing.

"Can you believe him?" Janet said in a breathless screech. "The nerve!"

"I can't believe Aaron wouldn't even say hello," Jessica said, kicking angrily at the dirt. "What a bunch of jerks."

She heard footsteps behind them and turned to

see Steven coming up, his hands on his hips. "Jerks?" he repeated. "Well, what I see is a bunch of guys who are dedicated to their sport, determined to win, and willing to work really hard to do it."

Jessica frowned. She was really getting tired of listening to her brother pick on them.

"What am I seeing now?" Steven asked, gazing at each Honeybee. "A bunch of quitters? A bunch of girls who want to win only if it's easy? A team who's willing to let a bunch of guys show them up?"

Jessica bit her lip. *Quitter,* she repeated to herself. She hated the sound of that word. Was she really about to let a bunch of guys show her up—especially guys as stuck-up and obnoxious as the Wolverines?

She turned to Lila. "Well, are we just going to stand here and let him pick on us?"

"Umm, well . . ." Lila said hesitantly.

Jessica nudged her friend gently and turned to the rest of her teammates. "Of course we're not. This is a training session, for crying out loud! And we can train as hard as the Wolverines, right?"

Elizabeth gave her a small smile. "Right. Harder, in fact."

"Way harder," Mandy added.

"That's what I've been saying all along." Janet smiled sweetly at Steven. "Especially after Steven has worked so hard for us."

Jessica managed to stifle a snort. She trudged back onto the track. "So let's go! Last one around the track is a gym sock!"

Seven

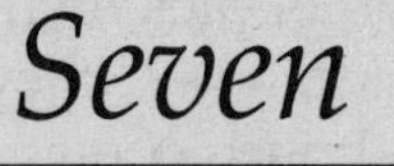

"How'd I do?" Janet asked breathlessly. It was Friday afternoon, and she'd just crossed the finish line on the outdoor track.

"Real good," Steven said approvingly. "You've taken forty seconds off your time from last Sunday." *Thanks to my coaching.*

Janet smiled at him, then ran off to get into formation for calisthenics.

Steven noted her time on his clipboard, where he'd been keeping track of everyone's progress. He planned to show this clipboard to Coach Berger, who'd of course be incredibly impressed at how professional Steven had been.

"OK, go!" Steven nodded for Amy to begin her sprint. She took off around the track at top speed.

"We're already a lot better—I can feel it," Jessica said behind him.

Steven kept his eyes on Amy, making mental notes about working with her on using her arms to help her run faster. That was the kind of thing coaches did. "Yeah, you are," he agreed. "I hope you don't forget who to thank for it. Keep it up, Amy!" he yelled through cupped hands. "Get those legs moving!" On the far side of the track, he could see Amy pour on extra speed.

He grinned to himself. No doubt about it—he was some coach. It hadn't even been a week yet. Before long, he'd turn the girls from the Tortoises into the Rockets, all by himself. Single-handedly. Then Coach Berger would have to give him that assistant coaching position. He would just have to.

"Looking good, Sutton!" he yelled.

"Oh, my gosh, I can't look," Julie muttered on Saturday afternoon, covering her face with her notebook.

"Julie." Elizabeth tugged on her shoulder. "You have to look. You're covering the game for the *Sixers*. Come on—Bruce is on the foul line, ready to shoot."

Elizabeth waited for his shot breathlessly, along with everyone on the Sweet Valley Middle School side of the gym. This game against the Weston Middle School Bulldogs had been neck and neck the whole way. Now the score was forty to thirty-nine, Bulldogs, and there were four seconds left in the game.

"If Bruce makes one foul shot, we'll tie," Elizabeth murmured, "and the game will go into overtime. If he makes both shots, the Wolverines will have their seventh victory in a row."

"I know, I know," Maria muttered nervously from her seat next to Julie.

And of course, Elizabeth added to herself, *if he misses both shots, the Wolverines' winning streak will be over.*

"Oh, gosh, there he goes," Julie said, waving her hand as Bruce bent his knees, preparing to make the shot.

On the sidelines, Elizabeth could see the Boosters shouting, "Bruce, Bruce, he's our man! If he can't do it, no one can!"

Suddenly Bruce tensed, then crouched, sprang into the air, and released the ball. It went in!

"Oh, geezum!" Julie cried, writing furiously in her notebook. "We're tied! I can't stand the suspense!"

Elizabeth chewed anxiously on her thumb, unable to speak.

Everyone in the bleachers behind Elizabeth and her friends roared happily, then immediately hushed as the referee threw Bruce the ball.

Once again Bruce took his position on the foul line.

Elizabeth tapped her foot to the rhythm of the Boosters' chant: "Go, Bruce! Go, Bruce! Go, Bruce!"

As before, Bruce concentrated on the hoop. He crouched, leaped, and shot. And it was in! Elizabeth jumped up with a gasp. The Wolverines had won, forty-one to forty!

In the bleachers, Julie and Maria grabbed Elizabeth and screamed as the gym erupted in cheers. On the court, the Wolverines heaved Bruce up onto their shoulders.

Elizabeth untangled herself from Julie and Maria and jumped up and down. Basketball had to be the most exciting sport in the world! Suddenly she realized how important it was for her to play well on the Honeybees—as exciting as it was just to root and cheer for the boys' team, she wanted to feel the same excitement that she knew the Wolverines were feeling right now.

She hugged Julie again, crushing her notebook between them, then hugged Maria again, too. "That'll be us someday," she promised, her eyes shining with excitement. "Someday soon."

"Bruce, you were amazing," Belinda told him at Casey's an hour later. Everyone had gathered at the ice cream parlor to celebrate the Wolverines' seventh big win in a row.

Bruce breathed on his fingernails and rubbed them against his shirt. "I know," he said. *Of course I was amazing. I'm a Patman. It's all in the genes.* Casually he took another sip of his chocolate milk shake and looked around. Tim Davis, the Wolverines' center, was standing next to him. They gave each other high fives.

"All right, Bruce," Tim said.

"All right, Tim," Bruce answered. "Good game, huh?"

Tim grinned. "You said it. It was a great game. Good thing you made those foul shots."

Bruce shrugged. "Yeah. I wasn't too worried, though."

"Yeah, no way could we lose," Tim laughed, slapping Bruce on the back.

"You guys played an amazing game," Janet said.

Bruce favored her with a smile. "We're the Wolverines," he pointed out. "We're unstoppable." Taking another sip of his milk shake, he smiled happily to himself. It really did feel great, winning. But then, it always felt great to win. Winning was something he did a lot of.

"Yo, Bruce," Ken Matthews said, coming up and shaking his hand. "Good game."

Bruce grinned. "It's always a good game—"

"—when the Wolverines play!" his teammates yelled in unison.

The Boosters and the other SVMS students began to clap and whistle all over again.

Bruce smiled and tried to look modest. He knew what everyone was probably thinking. They were thinking, "Thanks to Bruce Patman." His teammates were glad he was on their team, because it took some of the pressure off: They knew he'd always come through. Everyone else was just impressed with him in general. He sighed. Sometimes it was hard, living up to everyone's expectations of greatness. *Just part of the burden of belonging to one of the leading families in town, I guess.*

"Hey, Bruce?"

Bruce looked up to see Jessica, still in her Booster uniform, standing by his booth. A bunch of her friends were standing with her.

"Yeah?" he said, stirring his milk shake. Jessica always gave him a pain—like when she'd butted into that game of Horse at the park.

"Good game," she said, smiling.

He looked at her suspiciously. "Uh-huh."

"There's nothing like a good basketball game," Jessica continued cheerfully. "Did you hear how everyone was cheering?"

"Uh-huh."

"I can't wait to have everyone cheering for us on Tuesday." She smiled at Bruce, Ken, Aaron, and Todd. "You guys be sure to yell really loudly, OK?"

There she goes again. Speaking in code. "What are you talking about?" Bruce asked. "What happens on Tuesday?"

"It's our next game," Maria reminded him. "You know, the Honeybees. We're playing against the Johnson Middle School Violets next Tuesday."

Bruce stared at her. "Yeah, so?"

Janet laughed. "So you guys should really cheer for us. In the stands."

"Cheer for you?" Bruce felt confused. "You mean, like, at your game?"

"Yeah." A tiny line formed between Janet's eyebrows. "You guys were planning on coming to our game, weren't you?" She looked at each of the Wolverines at Bruce's booth and nearby. "We came to your game."

Bruce was speechless. Did these lamebrains really expect the Wolverines to appear at their pathetic girls' game? These babes were more deluded than he'd thought.

"What does that have to do with anything?" Tim Davis asked. "Everyone comes to a Wolverines game."

Jessica put her hands on her hips. "And now everyone is going to start coming to Honeybees games, too. Right?"

"No way." Bruce frowned.

"What?" Jessica's blue-green eyes widened. "Why not?"

"Why not?" Bruce echoed. "Is this a trick question? I mean, we're talking about girls' sports, right? The two words don't even go together."

"I guess you're forgetting that I beat you at Horse last week!" Jessica cried, folding her arms over her chest.

"Oh, please," Bruce scoffed. "I let you win."

"What?" Elizabeth demanded.

Bruce looked at Elizabeth patiently. "You heard me," he said. "Anyway, why should we come? I understand the gym didn't need cleaning for a week after Palisades got through mopping the floor with you."

Tim and Ken snickered softly. Bruce grinned. Patmans always did have a way with words. "Look, Wakefield," he said to Elizabeth, "I—and the rest of the Wolverines—have got better things to do than come to a silly Bumblebees game."

"That's *Honeybees,"* Elizabeth said through clenched teeth. "And what do you have to do that's so important?"

Bruce pretended to think for a moment. He put

one hand on his chin and looked up at the ceiling. "Like, floss, maybe."

"I don't believe this!" Elizabeth exclaimed, her eyes narrowing in anger.

"I'm outta here," Maria said bitterly.

"Right behind you," Jessica snapped.

Elizabeth banged the sundae bowl she was holding on the table, then stomped out behind the rest of the girls.

Looking after them, Bruce shook his head. *Girls are always one step away from being hysterical,* he thought.

Eight

"Go, Honeybees!" Steven shouted through cupped hands. "Go, go, go!"

On the court, Janet dribbled the ball quickly across the half-court line, then passed it to Lila, who passed it to Elizabeth. Breathing hard, Elizabeth leaped for a layup shot. She made it!

"All right, Elizabeth!" Steven yelled. While everyone trotted back, Elizabeth glanced over to the SVMS side of the gym and saw Steven pacing back and forth in front of their bleachers. Besides the six Honeybees sitting on the bench, waiting to be put into the game, there were only about four or five other people in the bleachers. On the Johnson Violets' side, the bleachers were packed with fans and parents.

Elizabeth gritted her teeth and ran down the court to get into position. The Johnson Middle School

Violets were playing really well, but so were the Honeybees. In just nine days, the Honeybees had improved a hundred percent. But as Elizabeth pounded down the court in a fast break, she feared that all their hard work didn't amount to enough to defeat the Violets.

A Violets guard tried for a jump shot, but Janet batted it out of the way. Unfortunately, Lila ran into the guard just then, almost knocking her down, and the Violets got to take two foul shots. The score was twenty-two to fifteen, Violets. The player made one of the foul shots, bringing the score to twenty-three to fifteen.

As the halftime buzzer sounded, Elizabeth sighed with relief. At least she could sit down for a couple minutes. As she walked back to the bench, she looked up at the bleachers again. Five people. She shook her head sadly and sat down as the rest of the Honeybees and Steven joined her.

"OK, guys, listen up," Steven said, walking back and forth in front of their bench. "You're all doing great. Janet, you're really on top of things. Jess, that was a great long shot you made."

"But it didn't go in," Jessica reminded him. She wiped her face with a clean white towel.

"It was still a great try," Steven said. "I'm sure next time it'll go in."

Jessica sighed and slumped.

Elizabeth wanted to think positively, but she was having a tough time looking on the bright side of the situation. After all the Honeybees' hard work, it looked as though the Violets were still going to win. And judging by the looks on her teammates' faces, they were just as bummed out as she was.

Steven came closer and put one foot up on the bench. "Ladies," he said, "I know what you must be feeling right now."

"No, you don't," Amy said morosely.

"Yes, I do," Steven insisted. "Remember, I'm on a basketball team myself. I know what it's like to play your guts out and lose anyway. But I think you guys are giving up too soon. You're really playing great."

"Steven, have you looked at the score?" Maria asked. "They're way ahead. They're going to keep on pulling ahead until they totally cream us. Face the facts."

"No," Steven said sharply, pointing his finger at Maria. "*You* face the facts. The fact is, this game isn't over yet. In some ways, this game is more important than the last one. No one was surprised that you lost your very first game. But how you play today will give people an idea of your potential, your future. It would be great if you won today, but that's not the point. What's important is that you play your best and not give up too soon. Your future as Honeybees depends on it."

Elizabeth looked meekly up at her brother. It was almost impossible to believe, but he really sounded as though he cared about the Honeybees.

"Today you all have to go back out there and fight the good fight," Steven said, meeting each of their eyes. "You have to show that the Honeybees mean business. You're athletes. Your game is basketball. Show them how it should be played."

Elizabeth sat up straighter, feeling a shiver run down her spine. She had to admit, Steven's words were actually pretty inspiring.

"What do you say, guys?" Steven asked, making one hand into a fist and thumping it into his palm. "I know we don't have a bleacher full of fans. I know we don't have a bunch of cheerleaders. But I still say you should give it your best shot. I still say the Honeybees are the best. I still say you should go out there and stomp those Violets into the ground!"

"Yes!" Janet cried, jumping off the bench and punching her fist into the air. "Steven's right—as usual. We can do it! Let's go get 'em, guys!"

Jessica's eyes were suddenly bright. "You said it."

As the play buzzer sounded, Elizabeth and her teammates rushed to take their places on the court. She and Jessica grinned at each other as the referee put the ball into play. And the second half of the game began.

"Man, two points," Amy said, shaking her head. "Two lousy points."

Jessica nodded. "Yeah, if we'd made just one more basket, we would have tied." She took a bite of her sundae. She and the rest of the Honeybees had gone to Casey's after the game. All of her muscles felt limp and tired, but it was a good feeling. She knew she had played well today.

"Compared to the game against Palisades," Maria said, "we were stars."

"It's true," Elizabeth said. "We really did play a mean, hard game of basketball."

"The thing is," Jessica said, waving her spoon, "the thing is, we *could* have won." *We came so close.*

"Next time we'll win," Janet predicted, licking her ice cream cone.

"Definitely," Ellen agreed, bouncing in her seat.

Jessica gazed thoughtfully at the far corner of the ice cream parlor. "You know, I bet if we'd had some fans in the bleachers, we would have won. I mean, we played so much better when just Steven was rooting for us, think of how great we could have played if the whole school was behind us, cheering us on." For an instant, she pictured the crowd yelling, "Jessica! Jessica!"

"Yeah," Elizabeth agreed. "The way we are at Wolverines' games. They have the whole school cheering for them, and the Boosters, too."

"And we have nothing and nobody," Lila said glumly.

Jessica snapped out of her daydream. "It's really not fair, you know? We've been going to every Wolverines game—not just the Boosters, but all of us."

Elizabeth frowned. "And I always advertise their games in the *Sixers*."

"I always cover their games and do interviews and everything," Julie said, her eyes narrowing.

"We come up with special cheers," Janet added indignantly.

"And what have they done for us?" Maria demanded.

"Nothing!" the Honeybees cried with one voice.

"Well, I for one have had it," Jessica declared, throwing down her napkin.

"What are you going to do, Jessica?" Lila asked.

Jessica pushed up her sleeves and clenched her hands into fists. "I bet those snakes are still at practice. Come with me and find out."

"Oh, come on," Aaron said, dribbling the basketball. He looked into Jessica's eyes. "You must be kidding."

"Nope," Jessica said coolly. "You heard me. If you guys don't come to our next game, you can forget about the Boosters at *your* next game." Jessica felt a teensy bit bad about being so tough with Aaron. She figured that if it was up to just him, he would come to the Honeybees' games. But Bruce made sure that all the boys followed whatever he said. Boys were incredibly stupid that way.

"And not just the Boosters," Elizabeth added. "But all the rest of us, too. Fair is fair. If we come to your games, you should come to ours."

"But how can you compare Wolverines' to girls' basketball?" Tim asked. "That's like comparing apples and oranges. It just doesn't work."

"What do you mean by that?" Janet cried angrily. "They're both team sports, they both use a round orange ball, they're both played on courts! How are they different?"

Go, Janet, Jessica thought admiringly. Sometimes she

could really see why Janet was the Unicorns' president.

Bruce rolled his eyes. "Oh, come on," he said.

Jessica could feel steam starting to come out of her ears.

"Think about it," Bruce said with mock patience. "It'd be like everyone going to see a boys' knitting contest. There just isn't a point."

Jessica felt as if she were about to explode. "Fine," she spit out. "If that's how you all feel, then I guess there's no point for the Boosters to cheer at your next game."

Bruce sighed wearily. "Well, whatever."

"And the rest of us won't come and cheer in the stands, either," Maria added.

Bruce shrugged. "We'll miss you," he said in an unconcerned voice.

"You'll be sorry," Ellen warned.

Bruce chuckled lightly. "Geez, you're making it sound like without you girls jumping around shaking your pom-poms, the Wolverines are going to lose or something."

Jessica's jaw clenched. "Maybe you will," she said tersely. "You don't give the Boosters enough credit. We always get the crowd involved in the game. Maybe that makes you play better."

"Yeah, right, we need the *Boosters*." Bruce laughed. He looked around at his teammates. "The Wolverines are lost without the Boosters, right, guys?" The other boys started laughing, too.

Jessica felt her face heat up. "Fine. The boycott is officially on. We won't come back until you beg us to!"

"Suit yourself," Bruce said coldly.

Nine

◇

Bruce crouched at mid-court, holding the ball tightly. He waited to hear the crowd roaring his name, as they always did when he was about to make a basket, but all he heard was scattered, unorganized applause. For a split second, he wondered why the Boosters weren't going into their "Bruce, Bruce, he's our man" routine.

Oh, yeah. I forgot. The Boosters weren't showing up for this game. Setting his jaw with determination, he sprang into the air, lobbing the ball at the Kings' backboard. It bounced off the backboard and missed the basket entirely. A JFK King grabbed it and tore off down the court. Bruce could feel his face redden with embarrassment as a few groans of disappointment filtered onto the court.

Where are those stupid Boosters?

* * *

"OK, men, what's the problem?" Coach Cassels asked the Wolverines at halftime. "The spark has gone out of your playing. Wilkins, your defense has been weak. Patman, your concentration is nowhere. Matthews, you missed both of those foul shots. Now, what's going on?"

Bruce looked down at his sneakers. The coach was right. So far, this game had stunk. It was hard to believe, since *he* was playing. "It's only the first half," he said. "We'll make it up in the second half. We're just getting a slow start today."

"A slow start?" Coach Cassels repeated. "That's one way of putting it. Another way to put it is that the JFK Kings are trouncing you."

Bruce had never seen Coach Cassels look so tense. Watching the coach pacing in front of their bench, Bruce had a strange feeling in his stomach—a feeling sort of like embarrassment, sort of like panic.

Finally Coach Cassels stopped pacing. "OK, guys," he began, and he sounded calmer. "Maybe you're just having an off day. It happens to every team. It's no big deal. You've had a great seven-game streak, but that doesn't mean it has to go on forever. Just go out there and do your best."

Bruce stared at Coach Cassels. It sounded as if he thought they were going to lose! He couldn't believe it. "Coach, we're the Wolverines, remember?" Bruce said. "We're the best. We're just having a slow start today, that's all. Right, guys?" He looked at his teammates, who were all studying their feet or their hands.

"Right, guys?" Bruce repeated loudly.

Tim nodded slowly. Rick Hunter shrugged. Todd rubbed his palms on the sides of his shorts.

"Uh, sure," Ken said.

Coach Cassels gazed steadily at his team. "OK. Two more minutes of halftime, men. Try to focus."

Bruce sat back on the bench and tried to clear his mind of everything except basketball. On the court in front of him, the John F. Kennedy cheerleaders were doing their routine. Their bleachers were packed with fans, who were clapping and stamping their feet. In back of Bruce, the SVMS bleachers looked almost as full as usual. Almost, but not quite. There hadn't been an article in the *Sixers* urging everyone to go to the game. And the Boosters weren't out on the court cheering, getting the crowd to go crazy.

Bruce shook his head. *Who cares?* he thought. *So what?*

Then he heard it. It came from the SVMS bleachers. Slowly he turned and met Tim's eyes. And they both heard it.

"Bring on the Boosters!" someone was yelling.

"Yeah! Where are our cheerleaders?" another boy yelled.

"Boosters! Boosters!" a guy chanted.

I bet that loser Jessica Wakefield arranged for them to do that, Bruce thought sourly. *No way are they doing it on their own.*

The halftime buzzer sounded again, and the Wolverines jumped up and rushed back onto the court. Bruce ran to his position and crouched down, getting ready for anything. No way were the JFK

Kings going to win today. The Wolverines would rally, Bruce knew they would. They would have their eighth winning game.

"So much for our winning streak," Aaron mumbled in the locker room after the game.

Bruce pulled off his sweatsocks and threw them into his locker. As he had predicted, the Wolverines had done better in the second half, but the JFK Kings had still won by six points.

"So much for the mighty Wolverines," Todd said bitterly, wiping the sweat off his face.

"I don't get it," Rick said. "We stank today. I don't know what was wrong with us."

"Me neither," Ken said. "I mean, last Saturday we crushed the Weston Bulldogs. And yesterday we had a fantastic practice. What happened between now and then? Nothing. We're the same team we were last week. Nothing was different."

"Nothing, except . . ." Todd's voice trailed off.

Bruce turned to look at him. He thought Todd was pretty much a henpecked wimp, but Bruce had to admit he was a good basketball player. "What?" Bruce asked. "What was different?"

"No cheerleaders," Todd said flatly, splashing water on his face. "The Boosters weren't there for the first time all season."

Anger flowed through Bruce like electricity. "You've got to be kidding," he snapped. "You're not saying we lost because some bouncy airheads forgot to show up today, are you?"

"They didn't forget," Aaron reminded him. "They didn't show up on purpose. And they're not ever coming back. Because we won't go to their games."

Bruce stood up and shoved his damp uniform into his gym bag. "You guys are nuts," he said shortly. "The Wolverines don't depend on the Boosters to win. We just had an off day, like Coach said. Next time we'll win."

Bruce slammed out of the gym without waiting for a reply. He knew there was no way the Boosters had helped the Wolverines win all those times. So they hadn't been cheering his name. So what? He'd just had a little slump, that's all. It had nothing to do with the Boosters. Nothing at all.

"I want ten push-ups!" Steven yelled. "Right now! Drop!" He blew his whistle as the Honeybees dropped, one by one, to the wet lawn beside the outdoor basketball court. A soft rain was falling, and dripping into Jessica's eyes.

Jessica stretched out full length on the soggy grass, then started doing push-ups. Next to her, Janet was moaning with each count.

"Come on, ladies," he called. "Straighten out, Wakefield!" He nudged Jessica's stomach with his sneaker. "The sooner you get through this, the sooner you can hit the mall."

"I'll be too tired to go to the mall after this," Lila complained, her thin arms straining to do a push-up. "And I'll never get the mud out from under my fingernails."

"So you'll get a new manicure," Steven said briskly. He clapped twice. "Now everybody sit up, feet wide. Time for stretches!" He blew his whistle again.

Jessica was soaked, but she couldn't tell if it was from rain or sweat. Her clothes clung to her, and her hair hung in limp ropes down her back. Splattered mud caked her sneakers and legs, and now her hands were muddy, too, from the push-ups.

"It's almost worth it," Jessica panted, "if it will help us beat the Big Mesa Bear Cubs on Wednesday."

"Yeah, I guess," Elizabeth gasped next to her. "Just once I'd like to actually win a game. Especially since the Wolverines' humiliating—hey!" She broke off as Steven nudged her lower to the ground.

"Uh-huh," Jessica said with a wicked grin. "It'll be great if we start winning and they keep losing."

"It'll happen, ladies," Steven said cheerfully. "Just trust me, and work your tails off. That's all I ask."

Jessica glanced over at Elizabeth. "You know, I think he's enjoying this."

"I think you're right," Elizabeth said.

"OK, enough chatter, ladies!" Steven said. "And one and two and three . . ."

"I feel like we're ready for anything," Amy said in the locker room on Wednesday afternoon, right before their third official game.

"We ought to be," Janet said, pulling her hair back into a ponytail. "What with running every morning before school and those extra after-school workouts."

Elizabeth looked proudly at her teammates.

"We're going to do great," she predicted. "And we should have more of an audience. The last *Sixers* was about practically nothing but the Honeybees."

There was a loud rapping on the girls' locker room door.

"Let's go, Honeybees!" Steven shouted. "It's time!"

Quickly Elizabeth joined the other Honeybees in a huddle.

"We're going to win," Elizabeth began.

"We're going to win," Maria said confidently.

"We're going to win," Janet repeated.

And maybe it really will come true, Elizabeth thought as each Honeybee repeated the chant. *Maybe it will.*

Heart pounding, Elizabeth shot the ball hard toward Janet, who threw it in a long arc to Jessica. *Come on, Jessica. Work it.* Jessica grabbed the ball, bounced it once, whirled to avoid a Bear Cub guard, and took one of her outside shots. It was in! Two more points for the Honeybees.

"All right!" Elizabeth cried.

Then one of the Cubs' guards took the ball off court and looked for a teammate to throw it to. Most of the Honeybees were pounding down the court to defend their basket, but Elizabeth hovered around the Cubs' center. And sure enough, the guard threw it right to the center. *Oh no, you don't. It's mine!* Elizabeth flung herself in front of the center and intercepted the ball. Almost before the Cubs knew what was happening, she had run up and made a layup shot. *Two more points for us!* The

Honeybees were in the lead now for the first time.

Once again Elizabeth and the Honeybees pounded down the court to defend their basket. The Cubs had the ball. Janet and Tamara, the two tallest members of the SVMS team, guarded their hoop fiercely, batting the Cubs' shots away. Then Ellen swooped in, grabbed the ball, and began dribbling it down to the Cubs' end.

Sitting on the bench during the fourth quarter, Elizabeth brushed the sweat off her forehead and smiled to herself. All the hard work Steven had made them do was paying off. Two weeks ago none of them would have had the stamina to last this long in a fierce game. Now it was the Cubs who looked ragged, while the Honeybees were holding up well.

Elizabeth felt her heart pounding with excitement. The score was thirty-eight to thirty-six, Honeybees.

We really might pull it off, she thought.

With two minutes left in the game, Steven tapped Elizabeth to go back onto the court, replacing Ellen. She took her position as one of the Cubs made two foul shots. The score was now tied again, forty-two to forty-two. *We can do it,* she chanted to herself, adrenaline pumping through her. *We can do it, we can do it.*

The seconds ticked down as the Cubs took their shot and missed. Jessica grabbed the ball and passed it to Maria. Maria dribbled it down the court, then passed it to Julie. Elizabeth was in the perfect spot for a jump shot, and Julie instantly threw her the ball. A Cubs guard immediately leaped in front of her, waving her arms, but Elizabeth sprang into the air and felt her hands release the ball. As if in slow motion, it sailed down the court toward the Cubs' basket. Elizabeth held her breath—she knew there weren't many seconds remaining on the clock. Then, almost at the exact same instant, the ball dropped through the chain mesh of the hoop, and the end-of-game buzzer sounded.

For a few moments Elizabeth had no idea of what had just happened. Then she heard an unfamiliar sound coming from the SVMS side of the bleachers—the sound of cheering. The twenty Honeybees fans were cheering wildly! The Honeybees had just won their very first game! Her last-second shot had made the difference!

"Elizabeth!" Jessica yelled, rushing over to grab her in a bear hug. "You did it! You won! We won our first game!"

"All right, Elizabeth!" Maria shouted, clapping Elizabeth on the back. "Way to go! Yay, Honeybees!"

Steven ran up to Elizabeth and whirled her around on the court so that her feet almost left the floor.

"You did it!" he cried. "You made that last shot! I can't believe it! We won, we won!"

A huge grin spread across Elizabeth's face as it all began to sink in. "We did it," she repeated, gazing happily at all her teammates. "We did it!"

Ten

"Yeah, and so then the Cubs' guard ran around me, trying to fake me out," Tamara was saying in Casey's an hour later. "But I leaned to the right, dribbled once, and passed the ball to Janet. And Janet practically dunked it, right there." Tamara demonstrated her moves to her rapt audience.

Jessica sat in her booth and happily slurped down her strawberry milk shake. Her teammates were reliving every moment of the game, and she was soaking it up. As Tamara and the others took turns recounting each play, each shot that had led them to victory, Jessica replayed them in her head, in full color. The entire game was burned into her memory in complete detail: She could see Janet leaping to make a layup and Tamara knocking the ball out of the hoop's path. She could see Maria dodging a Cubs guard and Lila swerving neatly past the

Cubs' defense. And then, of course, there was Elizabeth, springing into the air like a gazelle, delicately releasing the ball as if she were throwing a bridal bouquet. And the ball floated through the air, through the orange hoop, and down through the chain mesh. They had won.

Across the table from Jessica, Elizabeth gave her a big grin. "It was really—"

"Great." Jessica finished Elizabeth's sentence, then held up her hand. Elizabeth slapped her a hard high five.

Then Elizabeth sighed. "If only we'd—"

"Had our own cheerleaders," Jessica finished with a nod. "I know. I was thinking that during the game."

"You guys were way fabulous!" Mary Wallace yelled as she and Kimberly Haver rushed into Casey's.

"Hooray for the Honeybees!" Grace Oliver added as she and Winston squeezed into the booth next to Jessica.

"Thanks," Jessica said, scooting over to make room. Mary, Grace, and Kimberly were the only Unicorns who had decided not to join the Honeybees, and Grace, Winston, and Kimberly were what was left of the Boosters.

"Winston and I were thinking," Grace began. "You guys definitely need your own cheerleaders. We were all in the bleachers today, but I mean, you need people out there on the sidelines, urging you on."

"That *would* be nice," Elizabeth said. "But most of the Boosters are already on the Honeybees."

"Yeah, but there's still me, and Grace, and Kimberly. And Mary could join us, if she wants to," Winston said.

"I might do that," Mary said with a grin. "I mean, I don't have that much to do these days, since all the Unicorns are too busy for our regular club meetings."

"Good," Grace said, wiggling in her seat. "That makes four of us. We'll still call ourselves the Boosters, of course. Maybe Mary can borrow your uniform, Jessica."

"Sure," Jessica said enthusiastically. "It'll be great to have even four cheerleaders." She could already see them out on the sidelines, doing grapevines and jumps and even a small four-person pyramid. They would be chanting, "Jessica, Jessica, she's the one. Give her the ball and watch the fun!"

"Yeah," she continued. "I think that's a super—"

"Oh, please," came a pained voice from the booth in back of Jessica.

Jessica's eyes narrowed. She'd know that voice anywhere. *Bruce.*

Bruce turned around in his booth to face the Honeybees, his arms folded on the seat back. "You're not going to start on that again, are you, Wakefield?" he asked with a sneer. "I mean, your whole cheerleaders-being-indispensable theory. Why don't you give it a rest?"

"Why should I?" Jessica asked coolly. "It's already been proven. Fact: Without the Boosters, the Wolverines lost. Lost. Got creamed. Got wiped out.

Ate their dust. Got licked, beaten, cried uncle." She stood up, her hands on her hips.

Bruce looked at her darkly.

"Yes," Elizabeth chimed in. "After all, you guys were defeated, overwhelmed, crushed, steamrollered, bulldozed, clobbered. Whomped, subdued, skunked, conquered, vanquished, brought to your knees. Let's see—" She paused meditatively. "Am I forgetting something?"

"Yeah," Bruce snarled, wadding up his paper napkin and throwing it on his table. "You're forgetting who you're talking to, little girl."

"Oohh," Jessica said, batting her eyes. "I'm scared. I'm shaking in my high-tops. Aren't you scared, Elizabeth?" She turned big blue-green eyes toward her sister.

"Not really," Elizabeth said casually, taking a bite of ice cream. "Why should I be? He's only one of the defeated Wolverines, and *I'm* a Honeybee. And as you know, Jessica, we Honeybees are on a winning streak."

"*Someone* has to be," Jessica agreed, nodding.

"Very funny," Bruce ground out. He pointed a finger at Elizabeth. "But I have a newsflash, Wakefield. One win doesn't make a winning streak. I'm sure you'll be clobbered in your next game."

"We'll see," Elizabeth said airily. "But I doubt it. You see, we have *cheerleaders* now. We'll be unstoppable."

"Yeah, right." Bruce sneered, then stomped out of Casey's. As soon as he had gone, Elizabeth and Jessica burst into giggles.

"Wow, you guys really told him off," Maria said admiringly.

"That's my sister, the walking thesaurus," Jessica said proudly.

"Do we really have to be here?" Julie asked Elizabeth on Thursday afternoon.

Elizabeth nodded reluctantly. She and Julie were in the SVMS gym, preparing to cover the Wolverines' game for the *Sixers*. "As journalists, we should be objective. The *Sixers* is a school newspaper, and the Wolverines are a school team. So . . ." She rolled her eyes at the ceiling.

Julie nodded and flipped open her notebook. "We don't have to enjoy it, though," she said.

When the Wolverines trotted onto the court, Elizabeth and Julie didn't bother to stand up and yell their names, as they usually did. In fact, Elizabeth realized as she looked around, quite a few people weren't screaming as loudly as they usually did. And for the first time all season, there were actually some empty seats in the SVMS bleachers.

Their opposing team, the Johnson Middle School Jaguars, also trotted onto the court. Their side of the bleachers was only about half full—the Jaguars stunk, and everyone knew it.

"The Wolverines look pretty confident," Julie said.

"Well, just about anyone could beat the Jaguars," Elizabeth admitted. "They haven't won a game all season."

Julie nodded. "Their girls' team is definitely better than their boys' team."

"Yeah. This'll be a shoo-in," Elizabeth said.

"Oh, my gosh," Julie breathed. She turned and looked at Elizabeth, her eyes wide.

Elizabeth was pretty surprised, too. Todd had just totally missed a perfect layup shot—usually his best move.

"It's almost like they're cursed today or something," Julie said.

"It's weird," Elizabeth admitted. "I mean, after Bruce was so obnoxious, I was kind of hoping they'd lose, just to teach them a lesson. But I didn't think it would be like *this*."

"Yeah," Julie agreed. "How am I supposed to write about this for the *Sixers*? 'The Wolverines were completely and totally humiliated by the incredibly pathetic Jaguars on Thursday afternoon, when the notoriously bad team from Johnson Middle School managed to kick their tails all over the court.' I mean, there's going to be a riot or something."

Elizabeth sighed. "I have to admit, I feel bad for those guys." She shook her head. "To lose to the Jaguars . . . and by such a huge margin."

On the court, Bruce grabbed the ball out of midair and started racing down the court with it in a fast dribble, heading for the Jaguars' hoop. Elizabeth realized if he could make this two-point basket, the score would be thirty-six to eleven, Jaguars. Almost against her will, Elizabeth found herself hoping he would make it. *It just seems such a shame for Sweet Valley Middle School to become a laughingstock,* she thought.

But when Bruce was three-quarters of the way down the court, he suddenly tripped and fell. Elizabeth gasped as the basketball flew out of his hands, only to be grabbed by the Jaguars' point guard. She buried her head in her hands, then watched the game through her fingers as the guard ran in the opposite direction and passed the ball to a teammate. The Jaguars made another basket just as the final buzzer sounded.

"Wow," Julie whispered. "This is going to be a killer article." She looked down at her game notes. "Everyone made stupid mistakes. Bruce tripped. People's passes were off. A lot of balls teetered on the rim of the hoop and never went in."

In the stands behind Elizabeth and Julie, students were booing the Wolverines.

"What's wrong with you guys?" an angry voice shouted.

"Where are the Boosters?" an eighth-grade girl yelled.

"Yeah!" a third voice cried. "We need the Boosters!"

On the court, the Wolverines huddled together miserably. Elizabeth could hear Coach Cassels alternately scolding them and consoling them. Finally he gave Bruce a slap on the back and sent them off to the showers, his face grim. On the other side of the court, the Jaguars' fans were ecstatic with disbelieving joy and triumph over their team's first win all season.

Elizabeth and Julie looked at each other. "Looks like the Wolverines do need the Boosters, after all," Elizabeth said, clutching her notebook to her chest.

Julie nodded solemnly. "Looks that way."

Bruce tapped on the marble surface of the wet bar in his family's den.

"OK, OK," he said loudly. "Let's come to order, guys. You're all probably wondering why I called you here."

"To make us feel better?" Todd asked.

"No." Bruce rolled his eyes. It was Thursday evening, and he'd gathered his teammates at his house. Now they were lounging around the den after a swim and some hamburgers from the grill. "No, actually, I didn't ask you all over here so you could splash around in my pool and eat all my food. It's obvious that we need to do something, as a team."

"What do you mean?" Rick asked.

"I mean, today we lost to the most pathetic team in town!" Bruce practically shouted. He could feel his patience wearing thin. What did they think he meant? That they should all get together and sell Girl Scout cookies? "We need to get our act together," he continued, waving his hands in the air. "We've lost two games in a row, and one to the worst team in Sweet Valley. I mean, the Jaguars couldn't get close to a basketball if it jumped up and bit them. But they won today."

"They creamed us," Jerry McAllister admitted.

"Maybe we need to practice more," Ken suggested.

"Maybe we need to have the court resurfaced," Todd grumbled.

"We need to do *some*thing," Tim said anxiously. "At the rate we're going, we'll be out of the regionals in the first round."

"OK, let's make a plan," Bruce said briskly. He pulled out a sheet of paper and a pen. "Everyone come up with a suggestion, and then we'll decide what to do." He sat back on a bar stool, ready to write down what people said.

"That's a waste of time," Aaron said from where he was sprawled on the leather sofa.

Bruce swiveled on his stool to look at him, his eyes narrowed. He hated it when people questioned his suggestions. "What do you mean, a waste of time?" he asked impatiently. "You got a better idea, Dallas?" He crossed his arms over his chest.

"Look," Aaron said, spreading his hands wide, "it's not a question of practicing or having the court resurfaced or whatever. We're the same team we've always been. We can play just as good as we always did."

"Well," Todd said quietly.

"Well what?" Bruce snapped.

"Not good," Todd explained. "Well. We can play just as *well* as we always did."

Bruce rolled his eyes. "Thank you for that grammar lesson, *Ms.* Wilkins. Can we get back to our problem?"

"Our problem isn't *us*," Aaron continued. "Or actually, it's us but it isn't really our fault. I mean, it's us, and it's kind of our fault, but not really."

"Will you just spit it out, Dallas?" Bruce yelled.

"What I'm saying is, we need the Boosters," Aaron said.

There was silence in the Patman family room.

Then Bruce exploded. "Are you insane?" he shouted. "What do you mean, we need the Boosters? What do they have to do with anything?"

"A lot," Aaron said, jutting his jaw out stubbornly. "They're not just cheerleaders. I mean, they *are* just cheerleaders, but—"

"Oh, not again," Ken muttered. "Just say what you mean, Aaron."

Aaron took a deep breath. "I mean, it's not just their cheerleading that helps us. Though it does help us, a lot. But they really get the crowd riled up. I like hearing everyone in the stands yelling for us and cheering. When I hear the Boosters cheering my name, it makes me want to play harder, you know? So I won't let them down. The last two games, I haven't had that. It's depressing."

"Aaron's right," Todd said suddenly. "It's great to hear everyone in the bleachers yelling for us when we make a basket. And not only that—the *Sixers* hasn't been advertising our games like it usually does. And Julie had been doing player profiles in the newspaper, too. That kind of stuff gets people interested, and then they come to games. The more people you have in the stands, the more they yell, and the better you play."

Bruce rested his chin in his hand and considered. At first he'd though Aaron was coming up with one of his typical boneheaded Aaron ideas, but he had to admit, what he said had a weird kind of logic. It was true the stands hadn't been as full today. And it was true their fans hadn't been yelling as loudly as they usually did.

"Well, so now what?" Bruce asked testily. "They said they wouldn't come to any more games. So what can we do? We'll just have to play twice as good, that's all."

"Twice as well," Todd said.

"Will you shut up!" Bruce yelled at him.

"You know what we have to do," Rick said, looking around seriously at his teammates. "We have to ask them to come back."

"Oh, no way," Bruce said, shaking his head. "No way. That Jessica Wakefield is just looking for an excuse to stomp on us and humiliate us publicly. If we go begging to her now . . ." He didn't even like to think about it.

"If we don't, we're going to keep losing," Aaron said firmly. "Game after game. That's what I call public humiliation. Not to mention getting cut out of the regionals for the first time in Wolverines history. Our first regional game is tomorrow night. I say we need the Boosters, and we need them now."

Bruce sat silently as, one by one, his teammates nodded. He hated to admit it, but they just might have a point. It would kill him to have to go back to those stuck-up prisses and ask them to start coming to Wolverines games again, but what choice did they have?

"OK," he said brusquely, looking at the floor. "You all seem to think that we need the Boosters, for what reason I don't know." He tapped his fingers against the marble of the wet bar. "But I'll go along with the team majority, since after all, that's the kind of guy I am. So!" He cleared his throat. "Who's going to ask them?"

Todd turned and looked at Aaron. Aaron turned to look at Ken. Ken turned to look at Bruce.

"No way," Bruce said flatly. His eyes bored into Aaron's. Heads turned until everyone was looking at Aaron.

Aaron bristled. "We'll all go," he said. "All of us. We'll ask them at lunch tomorrow—most of them will be sitting at the Unicorner." Bruce knew that the Unicorner was a special table reserved for Unicorns. Since most of the Honeybees were also Unicorns, they'd be able to talk to a bunch of them at once.

"Fine," Bruce said, standing up. "We'll meet in front of the cafeteria at twelve-oh-five. Be there or be square."

Eleven

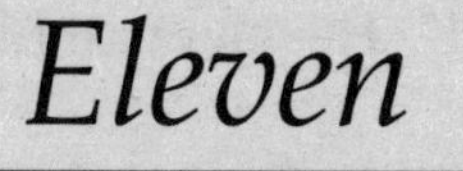

"Friday at last," Jessica groaned as she plopped her bag lunch down at the Unicorner table. "We can sleep in till seven tomorrow."

"Great," Janet said, popping the lid on her yogurt. "It'll practically seem like a holiday."

"You can't say the workouts haven't been paying off," Tamara said, eating a french fry. "Yesterday's practice was fabulous."

Belinda nodded. "I feel like we could beat a pro team."

"I bet we could," Jessica said proudly. She thought about how hard they'd been working. The Honeybees had to run two miles every day before school. They had a grueling practice every afternoon after school until dinnertime. Now Jessica felt lean and mean—a playing machine.

"I can't wait till Sunday," Mandy said. She took

a sip of juice. "Our very first regional game."

"Starring the wonderful, fabulous, incredible, and partly rookie Boosters," Jessica added, giving Mary Wallace a nudge.

Mary giggled. "I'll do my best to live up to all that."

"Ahem," came a voice in back of Jessica. She turned around to see Bruce, Aaron, Todd, Ken, Tim, Rick, Jerry, and the rest of the Wolverines standing in a cluster around the Unicorner.

"What do *you* guys want?" Jessica demanded.

"We, uh, we, uh," Aaron began.

Jessica snickered, then turned toward her lunch on the table. "How interesting."

"We'd like to ask you something," Todd blurted out.

Ellen noisily ate a chip. "So ask."

"We were all talking yesterday," Ken said. "You know, all of us Wolverines were. And we, uh, we decided, uh . . ."

"We decided that we missed the Boosters," Aaron said firmly.

"That's nice," Tamara said nonchalantly. "The Boosters sure don't miss you." She slurped her milk through her straw.

Jessica giggled.

"Well, umm, we miss you," Todd repeated, pressing on. "The Wolverines definitely miss the Boosters. And we were hoping, well—"

"Yes?" Lila prompted, a smirk on her face.

"We were hoping . . ." Jerry coughed, then looked helplessly at Bruce.

"We figured that if you guys wanted to come

back to our games, well, that would be OK with us," Bruce said reluctantly.

Jessica's eyes widened. He had to be kidding. "OK with you?" she repeated, staring at him. "Gee, that's big of you, Bruce. I'll tell you what—if we ever get the urge to come to one of your games again, we'll be sure to let you know."

"That's not what we meant," Aaron said quickly. "What we meant was . . ." He took a deep breath. "We, uh, would really appreciate it if you guys could come to our game tonight and cheer for us."

Jessica turned around again. She looked into Aaron's brown eyes, the eyes that could always make her melt.

"No," she said clearly.

"No?" Aaron repeated.

"No? Why not?" Todd cried.

"You know why," Janet snapped. "Because you won't come to the Honeybees' games. Besides, you guys don't really need us. You said so yourselves, remember?"

"We've changed our minds!" Aaron cried.

"About what?" Jessica asked, raising her eyebrow.

"About, umm, you know . . . not . . . umm, needing you," he stammered. "The Wolverines definitely play better when the Boosters are cheering for us."

"Tell us something we don't know." Lila sneered. "What else have you changed your minds about?"

Bruce rolled his eyes. "What are you talking about?"

"If we come to your games, you should come to ours," Janet said patiently, as though she were talking to a six-year-old.

"Oh, don't start that again," Bruce complained. Todd elbowed him sharply in the ribs. *"Oof!"*

"That sounds fair," Aaron said, giving them a big smile. "I'd like to come to a Honeybees game. I've *been* wanting to."

Jessica beamed.

"What about the rest of you?" Janet asked. "No Wolverines, no Boosters."

Janet can really make them squirm, Jessica thought admiringly. *What a Unicorn. What a Honeybee.*

One by one, the Wolverines nodded.

"We'll all come," Aaron confirmed. "If you guys come cheer tonight at our first regional game against the Palisades Panthers."

Jessica and Janet exchanged looks.

"We'll consider it," Janet said.

"Consider it!" Ken cried. "We have to know now!"

"I said, we'll consider it," Janet repeated icily. "We have to discuss it with the other Honeybees."

"When will we know for sure?" Todd asked anxiously.

Janet looked thoughtful. "Before the end of school."

"OK," Jerry said slowly. "We'll wait to hear from you."

* * *

"Crush the Panthers
"Make them cry!
"You can get
"Our score sky-high! Yay!"

"Gosh, the Boosters are really outdoing themselves," Julie said, stuffing some popcorn in her mouth.

Elizabeth nodded. "It's amazing, considering how little practice they've had lately. But they're just as good as ever."

On the court, Bruce raced past a Panthers guard and lobbed the basketball to Todd, who leaped up and practically dunked it through the hoop.

Elizabeth, Julie, Maria, and everyone in the SVMS stands jumped to their feet and screamed excitedly.

"Go, Wolverines!" Elizabeth yelled, punching her fist in the air. All around her the crowd roared its approval.

Todd and the other Wolverines rushed down the court in a fast break, and Tim Davis stole the ball from the Panthers' center. Then he dribbled quickly down the court to make another basket for the Wolverines.

Again Elizabeth, Julie, and Maria jumped up, cheering and clapping.

"Now, this is more like it," Maria said, not taking her eyes off the game. "I was so embarrassed when they lost to the Jaguars."

"Me too," Elizabeth said. "But it was their own fault."

"With the Boosters on their side, there's no way they can lose today," Julie predicted.

Elizabeth could see the Boosters on the sidelines, cheering every time a Wolverine scored points for their team.

> "Bruce, Bruce, he's our man!" they cried.
> "If he can't do it, Jerry can!
> "Jerry, Jerry, he's our man!
> "If he can't do it, Aaron can! Yay!"

Elizabeth gasped when a Panther took a shot at the Wolverines' hoop, but it didn't make it in. She held her breath as Todd grabbed the ball and passed it to Tim, who passed it to Ken, who made a great jump shot.

"Two more points!" Maria said. "Now it's thirty-four to twenty-six, Wolverines."

"I can't believe it," Elizabeth said. "Usually Ken's jump shots are way off. They're playing incredibly well today."

"It's the Boosters, I'm telling you," Julie said, taking notes for her *Sixers* article. "They've really whipped the crowd into a frenzy."

It was true, Elizabeth realized as she looked around her. With the Boosters on the sidelines, everyone in the stands was much more involved in the game.

"Listen to this," Julie said, quickly rereading her notes. " 'The Wolverines never played better than they did last Friday, during their first regional game.

The Palisades Panthers didn't know what hit them as the Wolverines pounded them mercilessly to a pulp on the court.'"

Elizabeth nodded approvingly. "Sounds great, Julie. Oh, look! Todd made both of those foul shots! Go, Wolverines! Yay, Todd! Way to go!"

"All right, Wolverines!" Jessica yelled with a last high-flying split kick.

The gym erupted in a roar as the Wolverines hoisted Ken up on their shoulders. The final score was forty-three to thirty, Wolverines.

Coach Cassels was out in the middle of the court, slapping all the guys on their backs and laughing and shaking hands.

Janet blew her hair off her face and tugged down her Boosters sweatshirt. "Whew!" she said. "I think we worked about as hard as the Wolverines did."

"I think you're right," Jessica said, flipping her hair over her shoulder as the Wolverines began to leave the court. "All right, Aaron," she called.

He turned. "Oh, hey, Jessica," he responded, smiling at her. "Great cheering."

Jessica smoothed her hair behind her ear. "Thanks," she said airily. "Just a few moves I—"

"Anyway, can you believe how they choked that move?" Aaron asked, turning toward Todd.

Jessica frowned. "Just a few moves I thought up at the spur of the moment," she mumbled to herself.

"Hey, Bruce!" Janet called, her eyes twinkling as he walked past. "So we'll see you on Sunday, right?"

"Huh? On Sunday?" Bruce asked, looking distracted.

"For our first regional game?" Jessica prompted.

"Game?" Bruce repeated. "What game?"

Jessica felt her stomach knot with rage. "The Honeybees'!" she and Janet exclaimed at the same time.

"Oh, yeah, sure," Bruce said, watching Aaron demonstrate a move. "Sure, no prob."

Janet peered after them. "Looks like the Wolverines have already forgotten that just this afternoon they were begging us to come cheer for them."

"Looks like they don't realize who was really responsible for their win today," Jessica agreed angrily.

"All I can say is, they better show up on Sunday, and they better yell loud," Lila said, gathering up her pom-poms with a flounce.

"Or else there's going to be trouble," Jessica promised darkly, watching Aaron's retreating back. "Big trouble."

Twelve

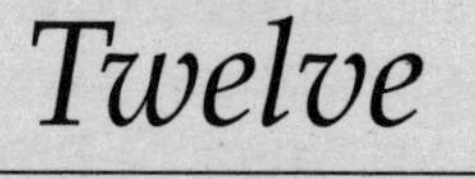

Elizabeth sat on the Honeybees' bench and hastily rebraided her long blond hair as she watched the court. It was Sunday afternoon, and Elizabeth was practically breathless with excitement over her team's first regional game, against the Weston Lady Bulldogs.

"What do you think of the game so far?" she asked Steven.

"I think you guys are doing great," Steven said warmly, his eyes locked on to the game. "Really great."

"The Lady Bulldogs are ahead," Ellen pointed out.

"Pshaw!" Steven waved his hand dismissively. "It's only the the first half of the game. And they're really good players with much more experience. You guys are doing terrific, holding your own." Steven quickly stepped up to the sideline and motioned with his arm. "Janet!" he bellowed. "Take it down, take it down!"

In response to his order, Janet grabbed the ball and began to dribble it down the court. Then she wheeled and shot the ball over to Belinda, who lobbed it to Lila. Lila grabbed it, spun, and threw it right back to Belinda, who jumped up and put it through the Bulldogs' hoop.

"Go, Belinda!" Elizabeth shouted, leaping up off the bench. Behind her, the bleachers were just more than half full, and Honeybees fans yelled their encouragement.

On the sidelines, Winston Egbert lifted Grace Oliver to his shoulders, and she waved her pom-poms high over her head.

Kimberly Haver leaned against Winston on one side, and Mary Wallace was on the other. They formed a big, vertical triangle.

"Go, Honeybees, fight, fight, fight!
"Our Honeybees have the might, might, might!"
"The other guys are running scared!
"'Cause Honeybees are out of sight, sight, sight!
Yay!"

"Those jerks," Julie said, fanning herself with a towel. "Look at them. They're totally embarrassed to be here. It's obvious."

Elizabeth turned to see the Wolverines slinking into the gym. At least, she thought they were the Wolverines. They were all wearing sunglasses and baseball caps pulled low over their faces, so it was a little hard to tell.

"I don't believe it," Elizabeth said, watching the guys slither up to the very top row of the bleachers. "The game started twenty minutes ago. They're just showing up now?"

"And what's the deal with the sunglasses?" Maria asked. "They can hardly even see the court!"

"It doesn't look like they're trying to see the court," Julie grumbled, watching the Wolverines talk and laugh among themselves.

"Hey, Jerry even brought a magazine, and he's reading it!" Amy exclaimed.

"Ladies!" Steven said sharply. "I want your minds on the game." He pointed to the court. "Pay attention to what's happening. Use your time on the bench to analyze the Lady Bulldogs, find their weaknesses. Elizabeth! What was the last play?"

Elizabeth bit her lip. Since the Wolverines' appearance, she'd lost track of her own game.

Steven looked at her sternly, then began pacing in front of their bench. "Listen up, ladies. You're in the middle of a game. Let everything else go. Keep your eyes forward and your mind on the action. Deal with everything else later. Is that clear?"

Elizabeth, Maria, Julie, Ellen, Mandy, and Amy all nodded.

Elizabeth glued her eyes on the court, determined to concentrate on the game.

But I'll deal with the Wolverines later, she swore silently. *Boy, will I deal with them.*

* * *

Sweat dripping into her eyes, Jessica waved her arms around the Lady Bulldogs' center she was guarding. The center kept looking for an open spot, obviously expecting she'd be passed the ball.

"Forget about it," Jessica hissed under her breath. "I'm all over you like ugly on an ape. No way is a ball getting through."

"Shut up," the center snapped back, narrowing her eyes.

Then it happened. A Lady Bulldog threw the ball to the center, but Jessica leaped up and batted it out of the way. Maria ran up behind her and grabbed the ball. Two seconds later she was making a layup shot right through the Bulldogs' hoop.

"All right!" Jessica whooped. "Go, Maria!"

With only one minute left in the game, the ball went to the Lady Bulldogs. Jessica could see Elizabeth moving in on the Bulldogs' point guard. Her twin's face looked grim and determined. The point guard threw the ball way over Elizabeth's head, and Jessica dashed over to guard the center. One Bulldog was dribbling her way to the Honeybees' basket, but Maria and Elizabeth were right on her heels. Jessica stayed with the center, ready to move if the ball came her way.

As if from nowhere, Lila darted in, snatched the ball out of midair, and dribbled halfway down the court. Jessica pounded over to the left in a pattern that Steven had drilled them on.

Like clockwork, Lila faked a pass to the left, then shot the ball over to Jessica on the right. There was a perfect, clear path to the basket, and Jessica coiled down, then sprang up. Just as she released the ball, the tall guard from the Lady Bulldogs barreled into her, accidentally-on-purpose. Jessica faltered, but the ball had already left her hands. It wobbled through the air, and bounced on the rim of the hoop. Jessica caught her balance and watched the ball. It seemed to teeter on the rim forever, rolling around and around for precious seconds. *Go through,* Jessica commanded silently. *Go through!* She sucked in her breath—and the ball went through the hoop! She had made it! With those two points for the Honeybees, the score was now thirty-six to thirty-six. There were seventeen seconds left in the game.

And Jessica had been fouled.

"Foul shots, Honeybees!" the referee called, pointing at Jessica. She went to the foul line, and the referee passed her the ball.

"You'll never make it," whispered a Lady Bulldog who stood close to her.

"You wish," Jessica whispered back. Aiming carefully, she jumped up and released the ball. But in her nervousness she overshot a little, and the ball bounced off the backboard and out onto the court without going through.

Jessica got the ball again and aimed carefully once more. A cold sweat beaded on her forehead as she stared at the orange hoop.

"Miss, miss, miss," the Lady Bulldog muttered.

Ignoring her, Jessica leaped up and released the ball. And it was in! The Honeybees were now one point ahead! At that second, the final buzzer sounded. The Honeybees had won! They had won their first regional game!

"Jessica! You're a hero!" Elizabeth shouted, rushing over and throwing her arms around her sister.

"Go, Jessica!" Lila yelled, waving her arms over her head.

Steven ran out onto the court. "You did it, little sister! The Honeybees are going to the championships!" he cried, swinging Jessica around.

Jessica beamed. "It was a team effort," she said. Steven had coached them all to say that, no matter who was actually responsible for the last point. "All the Honeybees worked really hard."

Jessica looked at the sidelines, where the Honeybees' four-member cheerleading team was jumping up and down and waving their pom-poms. Grace was running down the sidelines to do a high, snappy roundoff. Winston was walking on his hands, and Kimberly and Mary were doing cancan kicks.

And their other cheerleading section? Jessica whirled to face her teammates. "Where are the boys?" she asked. "Where are the Wolverines?"

Julie, who'd been sitting on the bench, shook her head. "They snuck out of the gym about five minutes ago," she reported. "They didn't even wait to see who won."

Jessica's jaw dropped open. "Those pigs!"

"But they left this for us," Amy said, holding out a card.

Jessica snatched the card from Amy's hand.

"'Come one, come all to the Wolverines' Victory Ball,'" she read, her eyes widening. "Seven o'clock Sunday evening at Bruce Patman's house."

"Yeah, right," Julie said.

"Like we'd really go to their stupid party," Lila added, glaring. "Let them have it all by themselves."

"Oh, no," Jessica said in a hard voice. "That's where you're wrong. We're definitely going to Bruce's party—all of us. And I bet it's going to turn into the most exciting party of the year."

"It is?" Julie asked, looking intrigued.

Jessica's eyes twinkled. "Trust me."

Thirteen

"Welcome, welcome," Bruce said jovially that evening as Jessica and Elizabeth arrived at his party.

"Hello, Bruce," Jessica said coolly.

"Step right this way," he said cheerfully, not seeming to realize anything was wrong. "Most of the party's out back, by the pool. Food's over here, and drinks are by the rose arbor. Let me know if you need anything." He moved away to greet some seventh-graders who had just shown up.

Lila and Maria joined the twins.

"Will you look at that?" Lila said, gesturing to a large banner that read CONGRATULATIONS, WOLVERINES! "They haven't even won the championship yet, and they're throwing this huge party."

"Yeah, they're really sure of themselves," Elizabeth said, pouring herself a glass of punch.

"Their game is next Wednesday, isn't it?" Janet asked, coming up behind Jessica.

Jessica nodded. "Too bad we won't be there to see them lose."

"This punch isn't bad," Lila said, taking a sip.

"Lila! How can you like the punch served by traitors?" Jessica demanded indignantly.

Lila shrugged. "Sorry. But Party Mongers are the best caterers in town. I love their punch."

"Look at them," Amy said, jerking her head over at where several of the Wolverines were talking loudly about their victory over the Panthers.

Maria rolled her eyes. "All they think about is them, them, them."

"You're right, Maria," Jessica said. "But I think it's about time they started thinking of us, us, us."

Jessica put down her glass of punch and squared her shoulders. With the Honeybees behind her, she marched over to the cluster of boys.

"I thought we were sunk," Aaron was saying, "but then Bruce ran up and grabbed the ball—"

"It's a great feeling, winning," Jessica broke in, smiling innocently.

Aaron smiled back at her. "It sure is. Gosh, I remember when Ken—"

"It was especially great when I made that foul shot at the last second, and we won our game," Jessica plowed on, a steely smile forming on her lips. "You know, our first regional game? Remember, today?"

"Uh, yeah, we know, Jessica. You guys, uh, played a good game." Aaron's eyes darted nervously over to Bruce.

"We played a *fantastic* game," Amy corrected him. "But you wouldn't know, would you? You guys came late and left early, before you even knew if we won or not."

Bruce shrugged. "I had to come home to do stuff for the party."

"Oh, come on, Bruce," Janet snapped. "You probably came home and watched TV while your housekeeper got everything ready."

"What does it matter?" Bruce asked, looking irritated. "We came, didn't we? And we invited you to our party, right? So what else do you want? Look, I even had them put your name on the cake."

He pointed over to the large sheet cake that was on a table by itself. In fancy, swirly letters, it read CONGRATULATIONS, SVMS WOLVERINES. Then, crowded to one side, in rickety letters Jessica could hardly make out, someone had added & BUMBLEBEES.

Jessica felt her face heat up as she glared at Bruce. "It's *Honeybees,* you dolt!" she yelled at Bruce. "*Honeybees!* You don't even know the name of our team!"

"It's close enough," Bruce said defensively, sighing deeply.

"No it's not!" Janet cried. "And you can just kiss your championship game good-bye, because the Boosters aren't setting foot in the gym again! Ever!"

"Oh, please," Bruce said, sounding bored. "Don't

start this again. It was a total coincidence that we won when you were there."

"It's always something with them," Jerry McAllister said impatiently.

"Without the Boosters, you guys don't have a chance," Jessica snarled. "You'll totally humiliate yourselves."

"I doubt it," Bruce said, examining his fingernails. "Not as much as we'd be humiliated going to one of your silly girls' games."

Jessica stifled a gasp. "That does it!" she barked. Leaning over, she dug her hand right into the victory cake. The icing squishing through her fingers felt cool and gooey. Scooping up a big handful, she threw it right into Bruce's face, watching it land on his forehead.

"Chocolate buttercream," she said snidely. "Your favorite."

Then Jessica turned on her heel and stomped over the patio, through his yard, and out the side gate. Just as she was turning onto the sidewalk, she peered at Bruce one last time.

He was wiping the icing off of his face. "Women!" he muttered. "Who needs 'em?"

You do, Buster, she thought angrily. *Just wait and see.*

"This is a disaster," Todd muttered as he and Bruce slowly moved in to guard one of the Big Mesa Grizzlies guards.

Bruce wiped the sweat from his forehead. They were only halfway through the first half of their championship game against Big Mesa, but it felt as if they'd been playing for hours. In fact, even though it was only Wednesday, this week had taken forever. And it was all the Bumblebees' fault, he thought. All week they had been holding demonstrations and organizing a Wolverine boycott. Now, today, the day the Wolverines had been working toward all season, the stands were barely half full. There were no Boosters, of course. The low energy level in the gym made it feel like a funeral. Bruce swallowed hard. The Wolverines' funeral.

"Quick, move!" Todd snapped, jolting Bruce out of his dark thoughts.

Bruce looked up to see the ball coming right at the Grizzly guard he was next to. Jumping up, Bruce tried to grab the ball, but his fingertips barely brushed it before the guard snatched it out of the air, then pounded down the court to the Wolverines' hoop. The guard passed it to another Grizzly who was waiting right beneath the basket, and with a neat layup shot the Grizzlies added two more points to their score. It was now twenty-eight to eighteen, Big Mesa. The SVMS fans in the bleachers booed.

Bruce clenched his fists, trying not to let the boos get to him. He had to keep his mind on the game.

Coach Cassels signaled Bruce to come out, and he sent Ken Matthews in to take his place. Unwilling to meet his coach's eye, Bruce came and plopped on the bench, then grabbed a towel to wipe the sweat off his face. With a sinking feeling, he saw that Coach Cassels was coming toward him.

"Patman," the coach said. "What's the matter, son?"

Bruce felt his stomach clench. When the coach called anyone "son," it meant things were really bad.

Bruce shrugged in embarrassment, looking at the ground. "The energy's really dead in here," he said, gesturing toward the stands.

"The energy's really dead on the court," the coach corrected him. "What's going on with you guys?"

Bruce shrugged again, his face burning self-consciously. "I don't know," he mumbled.

Just then Coach Cassels drew in his breath. "Rats!" he said sharply.

Looking up again, Bruce saw that Todd and the Grizzly center had collided hard in the middle of the court. Todd was picking himself up slowly, rubbing his knee. His elbow was bleeding from being scraped, and he limped off the court. The referee called two foul shots for the Grizzlies.

Bruce groaned. *Just what we need.*

"It wasn't my fault, Coach," Todd was saying as he limped over to the bench. "That guy fouled *me,* I swear."

Coach Cassels patted him on the back. "It doesn't matter, son," he said. "Get that elbow cleaned up."

Mutely Bruce met Todd's eyes. *Son.*

"This stinks," Aaron said softly at halftime, hanging his head down so the coach wouldn't hear him.

"No duh," Bruce said sarcastically.

"I don't know what's wrong with us," Ken agreed in a low voice. "We've never played so bad before."

"Badly," Todd corrected absently.

Bruce rolled his eyes. Someday he was going to punch Wilkins right in the nose.

"I guess the Big Mesa Grizzlies are going to be the champions this year," Jim said.

Bruce shot him a look. "They can't be," he spat out. "Everyone knows we're the best team. We've been the best all season!"

"Well, today we stink," Jerry said flatly. "And there's nothing we can do about it. The fans hate us. How are we supposed to play when our own fans can't stand us?"

Aaron's eyes flashed. "Hey, maybe—" Then he clamped his mouth shut.

"What is it, Dallas?" Bruce asked. "You got an idea?"

Aaron nodded doubtfully. "I think so," he said. "But it isn't pretty."

"Well, spit it out," Bruce snapped. "We're drowning here. Even one of your lamebrain ideas could make the difference." *As unbelievable as that thought is.*

Aaron took a deep breath. "The Boosters. The Boosters could change this game around. They could get everyone behind us, and raise the energy in here."

"Oh, no," Bruce groaned loudly, dropping his head into his hands.

"It's true, Bruce," Todd said firmly, nodding his head. "They could turn this game around."

"The *Boosters*?" Bruce said, his eyes wide. "You're dreaming. Anyway, they hate us. There's no way they'd come back. Even if we wanted them to. Which we don't. Right, guys?"

Ten pairs of Wolverine eyes stared at him, and Bruce got a sinking feeling in the pit of his stomach. "Oh, come on—"

Aaron raised his hand for silence. "All in favor of asking the Boosters to come help, raise your hand."

As Bruce watched, ten Wolverine hands went up into the air.

Bruce set his jaw. "Well, fine. Go beg for all I care. It won't matter—they won't come back."

"It isn't us they hate, Bruce," Ken said. "It's *you*. It's really up to you to convince them. Right, guys?"

Ten Wolverine heads nodded.

For several long moments, Bruce could feel his teammates' eyes on him, like lasers. He glanced up. The clock was ticking their time away, ticking away their championship. Then, taking a deep breath, Bruce understood what he had to do. It would mean making a huge sacrifice, but sometimes a Patman just had to do what a Patman had to do. He stood up.

"I'll be right back," he said.

Bruce found the Honeybees on the outdoor track. They were running with military precision. Steven was barking orders at them through a megaphone.

Bruce felt a jolt of surprise. *They don't look half bad. They're in pretty good shape. Running pretty hard without being winded.* Could it be that they were actually half-decent players? They seemed pretty together. He'd never seen girls look like this before.

"Fowler! Pick those feet up!" Steven yelled. "Miller! Sound off!"

As Bruce watched, Mandy came out of the ranks and ran alongside the block of Honeybees.

"Honeybees just can't be beat," she yelled.

"Honeybees just can't be beat," her teammates echoed.

"Not if we pick up our feet," Mandy yelled.

"Not if we pick up our feet," her teammates yelled in turn.

"We can dribble, we can shoot. We can give that team the boot!"

"We can dribble we can shoot. We can give that team the boot!"

"Hep, hep, hep, right, hep," Mandy called.

Bruce felt a vague surge of admiration. Then he shook his head. It was probably an illusion. These were *girls* he was talking about.

The Honeybees were running toward him, but none of them acknowledged his presence. It was as if he weren't even there.

Taking a deep breath, he held up his hand, then stepped right into their path. *It's showtime, folks.* "I have to talk to you!" he called.

"Ladies!" Steven yelled through his megaphone. "Take five!"

The Honeybees slowly came to a halt in front of Bruce.

"What do you want?" Jessica asked harshly, flipping her blond braid over her shoulder.

As he gazed at the Honeybees, Bruce understood

that the outcome of today's game depended completely on him. His teammates had all but lost hope. He was the only person who could turn the day around, who could change the outcome of the championship game. And it all depended on how well he could manipulate the Honeybees into giving in.

He dropped to his knees in front of the Honeybees and held out his hands. He'd seen someone do this in a movie once. It had worked.

"I was wrong," he said, doing his best to look sincere. The words tasted like sawdust in his throat, but he went on. "I was very wrong." He tried to make himself look like a poor, sad, lost puppy. In the rain. Alone.

Jessica looked at her fingernails. "Yeah, so?" she said casually.

Bruce's eyes widened. Didn't they know what they were getting here? How often did anyone get to see a Patman grovel? He should have known Wakefield would give him a hard time. He took a deep breath.

"I was wrong about not needing the Boosters," he repeated, opening his hands toward them.

"Uh-huh," Ellen said, looking at the sky in back of his head. "What's your point?"

Bruce swallowed hard. "Inside . . . today's game isn't going well," he admitted. "It's the championship game."

Janet tucked her T-shirt in neatly. "I wonder what's on TV tonight?" she said, looking at her teammates.

Bruce gritted his teeth. They weren't going to make this easy on him. "I was wondering . . ."

Tamara started whistling tunelessly, as if she were just killing time.

Time. The clock is ticking, Patman.

"We need you!" Bruce cried, holding his arms out at his sides. "We need the Boosters. We'll lose if you don't help." There. He had gotten it out. He tried hard to keep the sincere look on his face and opened his eyes wider. He thought about whimpering, but decided against it.

"What are you saying, exactly, Bruce?" Elizabeth asked.

"I'm saying—I'm asking, no, begging you to come inside and cheer," Bruce said, trying to look pitiful. He blinked hard several times. His knees were starting to hurt from kneeling so long. "Come help us," he continued. "Help us win the championship for Sweet Valley Middle School. Take pity on us." He tried to look as sad as he could. Should he even—sniffle? Nah.

The Honeybees looked at each other.

"No," Jessica said distinctly.

Bruce couldn't believe his ears. *"What?"*

"No," Janet echoed.

Bruce's eyes widened. "Huh?"

"No," Elizabeth repeated.

Bruce's jaw dropped open. "Oh, come on!" he snapped impatiently. "I'm begging you here. I'm on my knees. What's wrong with you people?"

The Honeybees just looked bored. Ellen leaned down and retied her sneaker.

"Look, we'll come to every single game you guys play," Bruce said desperately.

"The season's almost over," Lila pointed out.

"We'll cheer loudly," Bruce said, thinking fast. "We'll come early and leave late."

Maria yawned and scratched her leg.

"Come on," Bruce pleaded. "Halftime's almost over. Name your price."

"Hmm." Jessica got an evil glint in her eye. She motioned the Honeybees over, and they huddled together, their backs to him. He felt a pang of fear. He had a bad feeling about this.

Finally they turned back around. The look of triumph on their faces was terrible to see. Bruce swallowed hard.

"OK," Janet said, a frightening sneer on her face. "We'll make you a deal. An offer you can't refuse."

Fourteen

"Come on," Elizabeth said, climbing the bleachers ahead of Maria and Julie. The rest of the Honeybees had gone directly to the sidelines to begin cheering for the Wolverines. Elizabeth found them seats together, and they sat down.

"Do you think people will mind that they're not wearing their Booster costumes?" Julie asked.

Maria shook her head. "Nah. They're too relieved that the Boosters showed up at all."

Elizabeth could see that Janet, Jessica, Amy, and the rest of the Boosters had lined up on the side of the court. Even though they were all dressed in T-shirts and shorts, they had grabbed their pom-poms from the girls' locker room. Now they shook them vigorously over their heads, and Elizabeth felt a little thrill of excitement. Seeing them on the court, Grace Oliver, Kimberly, and

Winston ran down from the bleachers and joined them.

"Lean to the left!" the Boosters shouted.
"Lean to the right!
"Come on, Wolverines,
"Fight, fight, fight!"

Then the Boosters jumped up into split kicks, and cheered each Wolverine's name.

Up in the bleachers, Elizabeth was surrounded by fans who had suddenly perked up.

"Yay, Boosters!" Patrick Morris shouted.

"Go, Wolverines!" Charlie Cashman yelled.

"Beat Big Mesa!" Caroline Pearce screamed.

The halftime buzzer sounded again, and the Wolverines ran out on the court. They looked more cheerful, Elizabeth thought, starting to get tense with anticipation. She noticed that Todd had a bandage on his elbow, but it didn't seem to bother him. All the Wolverines were grinning at the Boosters, and slapping high fives with each other. Elizabeth saw Todd and Ken pat Bruce on the back.

She grinned at Maria, sitting next to her. "Looks like they're back."

"Uh-huh," Maria said, wiggling in her seat.

Then the game began again.

"Oh, nice shot, Tim," Maria said, her eyes on the game.

"Wow, did you see that jump?" Julie asked.

In no time at all the score was thirty-four to thirty,

Grizzlies. The Wolverines were catching up fast. Every time a Wolverine made points for their team or prevented a Grizzly from making points, the Boosters cheered loudly. Whenever there was a lull in the playing, the Boosters filled the gym with sounds of cheering and clapping. Their pom-poms were blue and white blurs. Their kicks had never been higher, their routines never bouncier or more energetic.

Elizabeth could see the Wolverines playing better and better. Their teamwork flowed more smoothly, their shots became more accurate, their jumps higher. Again and again they snatched the ball away from the Grizzlies; again and again the Wolverines scored.

Every time they scored, the fans in the bleachers jumped up and shouted happily, clapping and stomping their feet. Although the bleachers weren't even half full, their cheering filled the gym all the way up to the rafters.

Soon the score was forty to thirty-six, Wolverines.

"Looks like they just might win the championship after all," Elizabeth said.

"They're playing great," Julie declared. "It's like the Boosters have raised them from the dead or something."

Maria grinned wickedly. "I hope they think the price is worth it," she said. "Wait till they find out what Bruce promised us."

"First they'll thank him," Elizabeth said with a grin, "then they'll kill him."

* * *

"Wolverines once, Wolverines twice!
"Come on, boys, don't be so nice.
"Stomp those Grizzlies, make them moan
"Make sure you bring that trophy home! Yay,
Wolverines!"

Jessica shook her pom-poms hard over her head and smiled widely at the fans. She had to admit, she really did want SVMS to win over Big Mesa. The Big Mesa kids were total snobs.

Just then the crowd roared, and Jessica turned around in time to see Todd make a last, desperate jump shot. As the ball sank through the hoop, the final buzzer sounded. They had won the championship, forty-four to forty-two!

"All right!" Jessica shouted, jumping and waving her pom-poms over her head. Now the fans in the bleachers were going wild, storming the court and hugging all the players.

Coach Cassels was right in the middle of the crowd, hugging any player he could get close to. Jessica saw him clap Todd on the back, then shake hands with Tim.

"Bruce!" Coach Cassels called, surging through the crowd at him. "Excellent game. Well done."

"Oh, it was nothing, Coach." Bruce waved his hand dismissively. "I knew the Wolverines would come through."

Jessica shot him her fiercest glare.

Bruce caught sight of her and cleared his throat. "I mean, we really have the Boosters to thank," he said loudly. "The Boosters got the crowd behind us and helped us play our best. Yes, sir, without the Boosters this would have been a really ugly game."

Jessica smiled approvingly. Bruce wiped the sweat off his brow and grinned a little in relief.

"Come on, everyone!" he yelled over the roaring of the crowd. "Everyone come over to my house! We'll have another party—a *real* celebration party!"

"All right!" Jerry yelled, punching his fist in the air. "Let's all go to Patman's!"

"Oh, my gosh, I can't believe we're finally here," Lila moaned on Sunday afternoon in the girls' locker room.

Jessica nodded, pulling her long hair into a braid. *I can't believe it either.* Her heart felt like a drum beating inside her chest.

"I never thought we'd come this far," Tamara agreed, lacing her sneakers.

"These uniforms are fabulous," Belinda said, admiring herself in the mirror. "I don't care if we did totally wipe out our entire Unicorn treasury."

"Not to mention Mr. Fowler's contribution," Jessica pointed out, pulling her blue uniform tank top over her head. "Thanks, Lila."

Lila tossed her hair. "Daddy is always giving his money to good causes."

Jessica smiled to herself. Lila might have become a lean, mean, playing machine, but she was also—Lila.

"Ladies!" Steven burst into the girls' locker room, a black blindfold tied over his eyes.

Elizabeth grabbed a towel. "Get out of here, Steven!" she yelled.

The other Honeybees scrambled into their clothes or ducked into shower stalls or behind lockers.

Steven smirked, holding his arms out in front of him. "Relax, munchkin," he said. "I can't see a thing." He bumped into a stand of lockers. "Ouch. I just wanted to say that you guys are totally ready for this game today. The John F. Kennedy Queens are no match for you, and you're going to do great. Even though you've only been playing a few weeks, you've come much further than I thought you could. You've worked really hard, and I'm proud of you."

"Thanks, Steven," Jessica said. She looked around and saw that her teammates had finished dressing. Leaning over, she pulled Steven's blindfold off. "I don't know if I should admit this—but you've been a really great coach."

He grinned. "Thanks, kid." He clapped his hands. "Now, go out there and get 'em! Go stomp those Queens into the ground!"

"We have to do *what*?" Ken yelled, staring at Bruce in horror. "No way. No way. Forget about it."

"Bruce, I can't believe you would do this to us," Jerry said accusingly.

"Look, I told you. It was a life or death situation," Bruce said defensively. "I had to make a quick decision. And you know what the Honeybees are like: They could get blood from a stone."

"Blood, yeah," Todd said in disgust. "But *this*?

We'll never live it down, man." He shook his head.

Bruce stuck out his jaw. "Oh, I guess it would have been easier to live down our losing the regional championships, huh?" he snapped. "Get off it, Wilkins. We needed help, we got it. Now we have to pay the price."

"This is going to be bad," Aaron mumbled, staring down at their pile of equipment.

"Life's rough," Bruce said, tossing Aaron his uniform. "Suck it up."

Fifteen

"Honeybees! Honeybees!" the crowd chanted as the team ran onto the court. Jessica felt a thrill go through her as she trotted with her teammates to their bench.

"Finally, we have fans," Amy said happily.

"It's great," Jessica agreed. Behind them, flash-bulbs were popping and people were calling their names. She turned around and found her parents in the bleachers. They waved cheerfully at her, and her father made a V for victory sign.

"Too bad it took until our last game for everyone to wake up and smell the café au lait," Lila said.

Their rival team ran out onto the court, and the JFK side of the bleachers yelled in support.

Janet poked Jessica in the ribs and pointed to the gym doors. "Check it out," she breathed. "They did it. They actually did it."

A smile spread over Jessica's face as the Honeybees' cheerleaders slinked onto the court. At first there was confused buzzing from the stands. Then a moment of silence, then a huge, rolling wave of laughter, cheering, and clapping broke out from the stands and filled the gym.

"Wow, look at that," Jessica heard someone say.

"Get a load of those hot cheerleaders," a girl called.

Jessica smirked. The Honeybees' cheerleaders, the Drones, were dressed in bluish purple Booster sweatshirts, short, white pleated Booster skirts, and holding blue and white pom-poms. They huddled in a mortified circle at the end of the gym.

Lila turned to grin at Jessica. "They'll never forgive you for this," she said.

Jessica shrugged. "They'll get over it."

Maria cocked her head thoughtfully. "You know, the scary thing is that some of them actually look kind of cute in skirts. I never noticed what great legs Ken has."

As Jessica watched, the Drones started to perform their first cheer. They bunched together miserably, practically whispering "Lean to the left," and their pom-poms were hardly moving at all.

Jessica sighed. She would have to deal with them later.

"Elizabeth, out," Steven called, pointing to his watch. "Yo, Tamara."

"Can you believe this turnout?" Tamara panted

as she flopped next to Elizabeth on the bench. They were ten minutes into the game, and Steven had just replaced her with Maria. Elizabeth herself had started the game, but Mandy had taken her place a few minutes ago.

Elizabeth nodded, then giggled. "Oh, look, Bruce just bonked Jim on the head with a pom-pom."

"The Drones are better players than they are cheerleaders," Amy said with a smirk.

"Yeah, but somehow I'm enjoying their cheering more," Elizabeth mused.

The Kennedy coach called a time-out, and the Honeybees swarmed over to their bench, where Steven was handing out sports drinks.

"Don't drink too fast," he warned them. "You guys are doing great—Ellen, that was a good setup you made. Jessica, great jump shot, as usual. We have them on the run, ladies—we're already ahead, seven to three. Let's keep it up."

After she gulped down her drink, Jessica marched over to the Drones.

They cowered sullenly, hiding behind their pom-poms.

"Oh, no, you don't," she told them. "You guys don't get to hide in the corner. I want you front and center."

Jessica grabbed Aaron's hand and pulled him to the middle of the sidelines, right in front of the SVMS bleachers. She beckoned for the rest of the Drones to follow him.

"Now I want to hear some cheers," Jessica said firmly. She faced the bleachers and clapped her hands. "Listen up, everybody! The Drones have some cheers they want to do!"

Everyone in the stands clapped and laughed, and several people whistled and catcalled.

"Now, guys," Jessica instructed. "You need to put your hands together. You need to shake those pom-poms. You need to get those feet in the air in really big kicks. And"—she leaned over into Bruce's face—"you need to look like you're *enjoying* it."

Bruce's lip curled in an angry grimace, but he motioned to the other Drones to get in a line. Bruce led the Drones in a limp, clumsy grapevine.

"Honeybees once, Honeybees twice," they said weakly, staring at their shoes.

"Come on, girls, don't be so nice.

"Stomp those Queens and make them moan

"Make sure you bring that trophy home."

The fans went wild.

"Way to go, Drones!" Joe Howell shouted.

"Do it louder!" Sophia Rizzo cried.

"Yay, Honeybees!" Mary Wallace yelled.

Jessica smiled triumphantly. "Now that's more like it," she told the Drones, then sashayed back to the Honeybees' bench.

The ball was coming right at Jessica. She didn't have time to think. Leaping into the air, she grabbed it, then felt her sneakers hit the court. She whirled to the left, dodged a persistent Kennedy guard, and threw the ball. It bounced off the backboard, dangled on the rim, then finally, unbelievably, went through.

Janet ran over and slapped her a high five. "All right, Jessica!" she cried. "Now we're twenty to twelve. We're kicking their tails!"

On the sidelines, the Drones hopped up and down. Jessica gave them a meaningful look, and they jumped up a little more enthusiastically.

"Go, Jessica!" Aaron shouted, waving his pom-pom in the air.

"Miss it, miss it, miss it," Elizabeth heard Lila hiss as she guarded the Kennedy center.

The center looked unnerved for a second, then sprang up and threw the ball. It bounced off the rim and didn't go in.

"All right, Lila." Elizabeth slapped her a high five. It was pretty incredible, she thought. Before the Honeybees had formed, she and Lila had hardly two words to say to each other. Now they were a team, working together.

Mandy grabbed the ball and started dribbling to the other end of the court in a fast break. Elizabeth ran right behind her, defending her. Mandy passed the ball to Ellen, who passed it to Julie, who immediately passed it back to Ellen, who took an outside shot. And it was in!

"Way to go, Ellen!" Elizabeth jumped up and down excitedly.

The score was thirty-two to twenty-eight, Honeybees.

"Elizabeth, Elizabeth, she's the one
"She makes B-ball lots of fun!
"Janet, Janet, take your shot.
"Show those Queens that you are hot!"

The Drones jumped up and down, waving their pom-poms.

"They're kind of getting into it," Maria said, panting and resting her hands on her knees for a minute.

Elizabeth grinned. "They're actually pretty talented. And the crowd doesn't even seem to notice anymore that they're wearing skirts."

"Look at the expression on Bruce's face—can you believe he's smiling?" Maria marveled.

"Maybe he just likes winners." Elizabeth ran back onto the court.

This is it, Jessica told herself as she concentrated on the hoop in front of her. *This is what you've been working toward, all these weeks.* Throughout most of the game, the Honeybees had been comfortably ahead of the Kennedy Queens. Now there were eight seconds left in the game, and Jessica had a final foul shot to make. Even if she missed, the Honeybees would still win. But this was the final ball, and Jessica didn't want to be remembered as the girl who had flubbed the final basket in the championship game.

Slowly her calf muscles tensed. Her arms felt tired and practically limp. A trickle of sweat ran down her back. One damp strand of hair was tickling her cheek and making her crazy.

Then she coiled down like a jungle cat ready to spring. Then she jumped, her arms reaching forward, and she released the ball. It soared in a smooth arc toward the basket. At first it looked as if she had overshot it, but then, as though an unseen hand patted it downward, it suddenly stopped in midair and dropped through the mesh, not even touching the orange metal rim of the hoop.

She made it! The final buzzer sounded, and the stands erupted into deafening shouts and clapping and whistling. Jessica felt almost dizzy as her teammates surrounded her, clapping her on the back, hugging her, spinning her around. Steven pushed through the crowd, grabbed her hand, and raised it in the air. "My sister!" he shouted. "My sister made that shot!"

Bruce gave one final high kick, then rushed onto the court with the rest of the Drones. He couldn't believe it, but the Honeybees had come through. At least he had been cheering for the winners.

He saw Aaron race ahead of him. "All right, Jessica!" Aaron shouted, grabbing her and swinging her around. "Fantastic shot!"

"So you think girls can play seriously?" Jessica asked him with a smile.

"Hey, great basketball is great basketball, no matter who's playing," he replied.

Dallas almost has a point there, Bruce thought.

Next to him, Todd and Elizabeth shared a hug. "Congratulations," he said. "You played a great game. I was proud to cheer for you." Then he looked down at himself and frowned. "But I'll never forgive Jessica for making us wear these outfits."

"You did a great job," Elizabeth told him. "Thanks."

Todd threw his pom-poms up in the air. "Honeybees forever!" he yelled, and everyone took up the cry.

Bruce sighed. *Well, winners are winners.* He tossed his own pom-pom in the air. "Honeybees forever!"

Arms folded across his chest, Steven stood back and watched his team celebrate out on the court. In a few minutes, he would hustle them into the showers—it wasn't good for them to hang out in damp uniforms. They could get chilled.

But for now, he would let them enjoy their victory. Next season, he would work with them on some more complicated group moves, he decided, twisting his lip thoughtfully. Then he shook his head. What next season? He didn't even know if there would be a next season. He would have to wait and see.

In the meantime, he could sit back and enjoy his victory. And it *was* partly his victory, he thought proudly. He had taken a bunch of limp-wristed, out of shape wimps, and turned them into lean, mean, dunking machines. Every one of them could run two miles without getting out of breath. Every one of them could do twenty push-ups, and not the girly kind, either—real push-ups. Why, he remembered back when they had first begun training, they had been complaining about breaking their nails . . .

"Steven?"

Steven snapped out of his reverie. Looking up, he saw Coach Berger standing before him.

"Hey, Coach," Steven said. "Great game, huh?"

"It sure was," the coach agreed. "Am I to understand that you coached the Honeybees?"

"That's right," Steven said proudly. "I took raw clay and turned it into the Arch of Triumph."

"You did all right," the coach said, looking out on the court where the Honeybees and the Drones were still excitedly going over the game. "And it looks like you've gained valuable experience. Still interested in coaching the sixth-grade boys' team at basketball camp this summer?"

Steven nearly fell over. The coach was really offering him the job! Everything was working just as he'd planned! "That would be great." He smiled widely. Then he cleared his throat. "But, umm, do you have a girls' team I could coach?"

"I can't wait till next season," Elizabeth remarked to Jessica. The twins were having their own post-game celebration at Casey's.

"Me too." Jessica giggled. "Only maybe we'll

hold cheerleader auditions. Not just anyone can lead cheers for the Honeybees, you know."

Elizabeth laughed as Joe Carrey, their waiter, came over with their order. "Two extra-thick, extra-rich chocolate milk shakes for the champions!" Joe announced.

"Thanks, Joe," Elizabeth said, grinning. Joe was her favorite waiter. He was always cheerful, and he always made her milk shakes with extra ice cream. "Too bad you missed the game."

"I wish I could have made it, but I couldn't afford to take the afternoon off from work," Joe sighed. Then he cleared his throat and grinned. "But I'll be there next season, I promise."

As he moved away, Elizabeth looked worriedly at Jessica. "Am I imagining things, or did it look like something's bothering him?"

***Will Elizabeth find out what Joe Carrey's trying to hide? Find out in Sweet Valley Twins #96,* Elizabeth the Spy.**

Bantam Books in the SWEET VALLEY TWINS series.
Ask your bookseller for the books you have missed.

#1 BEST FRIENDS
#2 TEACHER'S PET
#3 THE HAUNTED HOUSE
#4 CHOOSING SIDES
#5 SNEAKING OUT
#6 THE NEW GIRL
#7 THREE'S A CROWD
#8 FIRST PLACE
#9 AGAINST THE RULES
#10 ONE OF THE GANG
#11 BURIED TREASURE
#12 KEEPING SECRETS
#13 STRETCHING THE TRUTH
#14 TUG OF WAR
#15 THE OLDER BOY
#16 SECOND BEST
#17 BOYS AGAINST GIRLS
#18 CENTER OF ATTENTION
#19 THE BULLY
#20 PLAYING HOOKY
#21 LEFT BEHIND
#22 OUT OF PLACE
#23 CLAIM TO FAME
#24 JUMPING TO CONCLUSIONS
#25 STANDING OUT
#26 TAKING CHARGE
#27 TEAMWORK
#28 APRIL FOOL!
#29 JESSICA AND THE BRAT ATTACK
#30 PRINCESS ELIZABETH
#31 JESSICA'S BAD IDEA
#32 JESSICA ON STAGE
#33 ELIZABETH'S NEW HERO
#34 JESSICA, THE ROCK STAR
#35 AMY'S PEN PAL
#36 MARY IS MISSING
#37 THE WAR BETWEEN THE TWINS
#38 LOIS STRIKES BACK
#39 JESSICA AND THE MONEY MIX-UP
#40 DANNY MEANS TROUBLE
#41 THE TWINS GET CAUGHT
#42 JESSICA'S SECRET
#43 ELIZABETH'S FIRST KISS
#44 AMY MOVES IN

Sweet Valley Twins Super Editions
#1 THE CLASS TRIP
#2 HOLIDAY MISCHIEF
#3 THE BIG CAMP SECRET
#4 THE UNICORNS GO HAWAIIAN
#5 LILA'S SECRET VALENTINE
#6 THE TWINS TAKE PARIS

Sweet Valley Twins Super Chiller Editions
#1 THE CHRISTMAS GHOST
#2 THE GHOST IN THE GRAVEYARD
#3 THE CARNIVAL GHOST
#4 THE GHOST IN THE BELL TOWER
#5 THE CURSE OF THE RUBY NECKLACE
#6 THE CURSE OF THE GOLDEN HEART
#7 THE HAUNTED BURIAL GROUND
#8 THE SECRET OF THE MAGIC PEN
#9 EVIL ELIZABETH

Sweet Valley Twins Magna Editions
THE MAGIC CHRISTMAS
BIG FOR CHRISTMAS
A CHRISTMAS WITHOUT ELIZABETH

#45 LUCY TAKES THE REINS
#46 MADEMOISELLE JESSICA
#47 JESSICA'S NEW LOOK
#48 MANDY MILLER FIGHTS BACK
#49 THE TWINS' LITTLE SISTER
#50 JESSICA AND THE SECRET STAR
#51 ELIZABETH THE IMPOSSIBLE
#52 BOOSTER BOYCOTT
#53 THE SLIME THAT ATE SWEET VALLEY
#54 THE BIG PARTY WEEKEND
#55 BROOKE AND HER ROCK-STAR MOM
#56 THE WAKEFIELDS STRIKE IT RICH
#57 BIG BROTHER'S IN LOVE!
#58 ELIZABETH AND THE ORPHANS
#59 BARNYARD BATTLE
#60 CIAO, SWEET VALLEY!
#61 JESSICA THE NERD
#62 SARAH'S DAD AND SOPHIA'S MOM
#63 POOR LILA!
#64 THE CHARM SCHOOL MYSTERY
#65 PATTY'S LAST DANCE
#66 THE GREAT BOYFRIEND SWITCH
#67 JESSICA THE THIEF
#68 THE MIDDLE SCHOOL GETS MARRIED
#69 WON'T SOMEONE HELP ANNA?
#70 PSYCHIC SISTERS
#71 JESSICA SAVES THE TREES
#72 THE LOVE POTION
#73 LILA'S MUSIC VIDEO
#74 ELIZABETH THE HERO
#75 JESSICA AND THE EARTHQUAKE
#76 YOURS FOR A DAY
#77 TODD RUNS AWAY
#78 STEVEN THE ZOMBIE
#79 JESSICA'S BLIND DATE
#80 THE GOSSIP WAR
#81 ROBBERY AT THE MALL
#82 STEVEN'S ENEMY
#83 AMY'S SECRET SISTER
#84 ROMEO AND 2 JULIETS
#85 ELIZABETH THE SEVENTH-GRADER
#86 IT CAN'T HAPPEN HERE
#87 THE MOTHER-DAUGHTER SWITCH
#88 STEVEN GETS EVEN
#89 JESSICA'S COOKIE DISASTER
#90 THE COUSIN WAR
#91 DEADLY VOYAGE
#92 ESCAPE FROM TERROR ISLAND
#93 THE INCREDIBLE MADAME JESSICA
#94 DON'T TALK TO BRIAN
#95 THE BATTLE OF THE CHEERLEADERS